# DEATH RIDER

The gunman was on a horse, and Fargo was on foot, running through mud. And as a shot whizzed past his ear, it sent him sprawling face forward into the muck. He was up immediately, unhurt, but when he reached for his Colt, it was coated with goop, and his hands were slick with it. Wiping his palms against his pants as he ran, it felt as though his whole body had been immersed in grease.

Fargo's gun was useless, his feet were slipping out from under him, and he heard the pounding hoofbeats of the gunman's horse coming closer and closer. Skye Fargo felt sure he was in a losing race against death. . . .

# THE TRAILSMAN 69

# CONFEDERATE CHALLENGE

by

## Jon Sharpe

Ⓞ

A SIGNET BOOK

**NEW AMERICAN LIBRARY**

*PUBLISHER'S NOTE*

This book is a work of fiction. Names, characters, places, and incidents either are the product of the author's imagination or are used fictitiously, and any resemblance to actual persons, living or dead, events, or locales is entirely coincidental.

NAL BOOKS ARE AVAILABLE AT QUANTITY DISCOUNTS
WHEN USED TO PROMOTE PRODUCTS OR SERVICES.
FOR INFORMATION PLEASE WRITE TO PREMIUM MARKETING DIVISION,
NEW AMERICAN LIBRARY, 1633 BROADWAY,
NEW YORK, NEW YORK 10019.

The first chapter of this book previously appeared in *Trapper Rampage*, the sixty-eighth volume in the series.

SIGNET TRADEMARK REG. U.S. PAT. OFF. AND FOREIGN COUNTRIES
REGISTERED TRADEMARK—MARCA REGISTRADA
HECHO EN CHICAGO, U.S.A.

SIGNET, SIGNET CLASSIC, MENTOR, ONYX, PLUME, MERIDIAN
AND NAL BOOKS are published by NAL PENGUIN INC.,
1633 Broadway, New York, New York 10019

First Printing, September, 1987

1 2 3 4 5 6 7 8 9

PRINTED IN THE UNITED STATES OF AMERICA

# The Trailsman

Beginnings . . . they bend the tree and they mark the man. Skye Fargo was born when he was eighteen. Terror was his midwife, vengeance his first cry. Killing spawned Skye Fargo, ruthless, cold-blooded murder. Out of the acrid smoke of gunpowder still hanging in the air, he rose, cried out a promise never forgotten.

The Trailsman, they began to call him, all across the West: searcher, scout, hunter, the man who could see where others only looked, his skills for hire but not his soul, the man who lived each day to the fullest, yet trailed each tomorrow. Skye Fargo, the Trailsman, the seeker who could take the wildness of a land and the wanting of a woman and make them his own.

*1860, far west in Kansas Territory,
where the Rocky Mountains rise from the Great Plains,
and men search for gold and excitement . . .*

# 1

Skye Fargo had ridden hard to arrive in the adjoining camps of Denver and Auraria City. The bad weather that had followed Fargo across five hundred miles of barren plains had settled into a cold, gray drizzle. And the avenues of these two fledgling Kansas Territory supply centers were mired in mud.

Since this new gold rush, there was some talk about turning this region into its own separately governed territory, although Fargo thought the idea a bit premature as his Ovaro wallowed in a river of muck. But the sounds of building—pounding, shouting, and cursing—greeted Fargo in spite of the dreary conditions. On both sides of the street, tents vied with freshly hewn, newly built, false-fronted buildings to create a chaotic, bustling business district.

With his jet-black fore and hind quarters stiff with drying mud and his brilliant white midsection stained brown, Fargo's handsome but weary Ovaro threaded his way between wagons and horses. Now that there was a definite gold strike up in Idaho Gulch, the future of Denver, or perhaps of Auraria City—the two towns were still fighting to take the lead— seemed assured. And men were pouring into the Front Range mining camps. It was said to be so crowded that men slept in shifts in the few available dwellings.

But Fargo had taken precautions. Waiting for him at the edge of the ramshackle downtown was a warm, dry cabin. It probably wasn't much, Fargo admitted to himself, since there didn't seem to be much to the infant twin cities, but at least he would have a quiet, private place to wash off and sleep off the residue of a long trek. From beneath the canvas awning of a restaurant tent, a man dashed out across a plank sidewalk, splashed in knee-deep mud, careened in front of a startled wagon team, and came to a halt next to Fargo's Ovaro.

"You Skye Fargo?" the man shouted, looking up into the stranger's lake-blue stare.

"Yes," Fargo answered.

The man's flushed face broke into a grin as he wiped his hand on the soiled apron he wore over his baggy trousers. "I'm Drew Dawson," the man said, extending a damp palm to shake Fargo's hand. "I can't believe you really got here so quick. But I done just what you asked in the letter. Sent my Sally over not an hour ago to start a fire and get a tubful of water heating. Place should be real cozy by now."

The man's eyes sparkled with excitement as he pumped Fargo's arm with an exuberance that would have toppled a lesser man from his horse. "So you come all the way from the Dakota lands since last week." Dawson shook his head disbelievingly. "See any redskins?"

"Yes," Fargo admitted.

"I hear them Sioux are pretty unpredictable. And the Cheyenne are right rambunctious nowadays. Did you shoot some?"

"Nope," Fargo denied, his tiredness giving way to an amused smile. "I guess I smelled too bad for them to get too close."

"Oh," the man sighed, reluctantly backing away as he accepted Fargo's hint. "You'll be wanting to settle in now, I suppose. The place is right on this street. Last cabin left." Dawson's eager grin returned. "Sally and me would be right pleased to have you to dinner tonight."

"I ate on the trail," Fargo told him. "Tonight I sleep. But I'm obliged for the invitation." Nudging the Ovaro, Fargo left the man behind.

The waiting cabin was a small, haphazardly built affair, its small stoop rising from a sea of mud, but from a precariously tilting stovepipe on the roof, a stream of welcoming blue wood smoke rose into the misty day, promising warmth. Before he went inside, Fargo led the Ovaro around back to where a trough and feed awaited. Then, feeling bone-weary and chilled to the core, with the grit of ten days' journey scratching under his damp clothing, Fargo waded back to the cabin door. Carrying his heavy saddle, he glanced around, but there was nowhere to set the saddle without drowning it, so Fargo kicked the door open.

The place was small and spare, furnished with nothing but

an old iron bed, a rough table, one straight-backed chair, a lantern, a large tub, and a huge fat-bellied stove with a big kettle of water simmering on top. But the cabin wasn't empty. A woman slept on his bed. The saddle thudded loudly when Fargo dropped it, and the woman sprang from the bed in one lithe motion.

"Oh, dear," she murmured, brushing at her skirts to straighten them. "I do beg your pardon, sir." Swinging around, the woman snatched her hat and gloves from the quilted spread.

She was the most incongruous sight Fargo had seen in a long time. The woman didn't sport hoops. But she was burdened with so many petticoats that they made her flounced yellow sprigged-muslin skirts cover nearly a fifth of the floor space available in the tiny cabin. Her hat trailed bright-yellow satin ribbons, and her white doeskin gloves could serve no possible purpose other than decoration.

For the life of him, Fargo couldn't figure out how she could have gotten to the stoop without trailing her jouncing skirts in six inches of mud. But she looked as fresh as a daisy, as if she were all ready to sit on the veranda of a Georgia plantation. And her voice was unmistakably southern.

"You Sally?" Fargo asked.

"No," she answered, looking momentarily confused. "I am Miss Amelia Miranda Parmeter." Abruptly she offered Fargo a coquettish, inveigling smile and held out one limp wrist as if she expected him to kiss her hand.

Fargo ignored it. Sinking back on the straight-backed chair, he began to tug off his boots. "If I'm not mistaken, that's my bed you were sleeping in, Miss Parmeter," he murmured.

"Oh, dear," she whispered. "I am sorry, Mr. Fargo. I merely came in because the weather is so horribly inhospitable."

"So you know who I am," he muttered, glancing up in time to see the woman blush.

Her elaborately pinned-up hair was slightly rumpled from her nap, and wisps of yellow curls tumbled down across her reddened cheeks. She pouted momentarily, then recovered, flashing a wholly beguiling smile. She was real pretty, and she obviously knew it.

Stripping off his socks, Fargo went back to ignoring her, but amusement danced in his lake-blue eyes.

"Of course I know who you are, sir," Amelia declared indignantly. "I've come to hire you."

"I'm already hired," he told her. "I'm leaving tomorrow. But if you'd like to stay until then . . ." Leaning back in the chair once again, Fargo flashed a smile every bit as beguiling as hers.

"Oh, do you mean it?" she blurted. "I would be most grateful, Mr. Fargo. I never dreamed that obtaining accommodations could be so vexatious in this desolate place. And this is so very much nicer than the tent I'm in. So dry," she enthused.

Startled, Fargo watched Amelia Parmeter pirouette around, looking at the dank little cabin as if it were a first-rate New Orleans hotel. He had only expected to see her blush again. "I don't intend to give up my bed," he protested.

"No, of course not," she agreed.

Her words woke him up as readily as a bucket of cold water. Grinning, Fargo rubbed his bearded jaw. "I guess I'd best take a bath," he commented.

"A bath?" she repeated, her eyes darting across the small confines of the cabin. "I suppose you'll want me to leave for a while," she said, sounding disappointed.

"You don't have to," Fargo assured her, suddenly feeling as if he had awoken from a long sleep. Fargo's blood pounded in his veins, eliminating all weariness. He stood up.

Amelia Parmeter was a pretty thing, little and dainty, and Fargo towered above her. She looked as if she were all dressed up to go to a ball, and abruptly Fargo smiled at the thought of layers of petticoats tossed aside one by one. It would kind of be like opening a Christmas present, he decided, and the occasion would be as rare, since not very many women dressed that way out West.

"Perhaps we should discuss my business matters first, sir," Amelia drawled softly.

Fargo dropped back onto the chair, all his weariness returning. "We have no business, Miss Parmeter. I leave for Utah in the morning."

"Oh, no, Mr. Fargo. I talked to Mr. Bentley and told him you wouldn't be available."

"You did what?" Fargo demanded.

"You needn't worry, sir. Mr. Bentley was most understanding. After all, you are the Trailsman, and Mr. Bentley only needed a guide. Mr. Bentley understood entirely why I required your services more than he did. And, of course," she concluded, "I repaid the gentleman's advance and found him a suitable replacement. A Mr. Davis. I believe you know him?"

Fargo gaped at her in astonishment. "Yeah, I know him. Josh Davis is fine. But it just so happens," Fargo said tightly, "I want to go to Utah. Don't you think you should have consulted me before changing my plans?"

"But, Mr. Fargo," she protested. Amelia Parmeter whirled away, her skirts swirling. She stalked to the head of the bed and fingered the iron bedpost distractedly before she turned away again and walked toward the stove, halting before her voluminous skirts came in contact with the hot metal. Finally, she faced him. She was young and restless and she had the tense edginess of a cornered animal. "Certainly, I didn't mean to insult you, sir. I fully intend to pay you twice what Mr. Bentley would." She swallowed. Glancing right and left, her eyes scanned the dimly lit room, until a shiver shook her shoulders as she forced herself to face Fargo again. "I was desperate," she whispered.

Fargo smiled tiredly. "I'm sure you were," he conceded. "Desperate and used to getting your own way. But it didn't give you the right to arrange my affairs."

"But, Mr. Fargo, I really must find my fiancé."

Fargo's expression hardened. "Goddammit, Miss Parmeter. I don't chase after errant husbands or fleeing fiancés. Since you seem to know enough about me to change all my plans, you should know that."

"Why, Mr. Fargo," she squealed. "You do me an injustice. Stephen certainly wasn't fleeing. He merely came out West to pursue his profession," she claimed, lifting her chin haughtily. "Stephen's a painter. And he did not leave me, sir. He merely took a trip. After all," she fumed, "our wedding isn't even scheduled to take place until after the first of next year." Amelia hesitated, eyeing Fargo accusingly. "And I'm going to find him," she concluded, her eyes suddenly shining with willfullness.

"Why?" Fargo questioned.

"Because I must," she answered.

"And you're not going to tell me why?"

"It's a personal matter," she said brusquely. "Surely, you don't need to know in order to find him, Mr. Fargo."

"I don't need to know anything about your fiancé," Fargo agreed, laughing. "Because I'm not looking for him."

"Oh," Amelia spat, spinning away again, her skirts sweeping out to take up almost all of the floor space between the bed and stove. She paced four steps, but there was little room for her theatrics, so she turned back on Fargo furiously. "A pox on you, sir," she shouted. "I shall not divulge personal information."

"And I'm not asking you to." Fargo laughed ribaldly. "I'm only here for the bath and the bed," he told her calmly. "If you want to share either one of them, you're welcome. As for your information, I don't want it." Fargo stood up and slipped out of his coat.

Amelia Parmeter gawked as Fargo tossed his coat across the table and began to unbutton his shirt, but she recovered quickly. Fargo could almost hear her mind calculating on the situation, clicking away like one of those little abacuses the Chinese shopkeepers in San Francisco used.

"Oh, Mr. Fargo, I am so sorry," she murmured, suddenly consumed by feminine vulnerability. Her hand fluttered at her breast and her wide blue eyes filled with tears. "I most certainly never meant to offend you," she pleaded.

He had no doubt of that. She meant to harness him and get him to do her bidding like some stupid draft animal. Unfortunately, he was too damned tired to outwit her, and too damned intrigued by her heaving bosom to just kick her out. Eyeing Amelia Parmeter sullenly, Fargo tugged his shirt out of the waistband of his trousers, knowing full well from the look on her face that she was about to attempt to postpone his overdue bath.

"You really shouldn't, Mr. Fargo," she murmured. "My brother will be here shortly and I'm afraid he would think your unclad state most improper."

"Your brother?" Fargo burst out, momentarily discon-

certed. ''So why in hell do I care what your brother thinks?''
he protested.

Amelia Parmeter stared at Fargo, looking genuinely puzzled. ''But, sir,'' she drawled softly, ''I am aware that
Westerners are much more lax in their manners than are
southern gentlemen, but certainly you have some idea of the
proprieties.''

Fargo shook his head as he erupted into laughter. He had
little experience with southern belles, and he was beginning
to thank his lucky stars for that.

''Listen,'' Amelia commanded. ''Why, it's Jeffrey,'' she
said, bustling to the door.

Amelia tugged the door open and leaned out, sending a
shock wave of cold outdoor air across Fargo's bare chest. He
shivered with irritation, clenching his fists to keep from
throttling the woman.

''Jeffrey, Plato,'' she called. Within two minutes two men
tromped into the room.

Younger than his sister, Jeffrey Parmeter shared her facial
features, and if anything, he was even more preposterously
dressed. His tight blue breeches were topped by a ruffled
linen shirt and a navy velvet waistcoat with satin trim. But his
high, polished boots were at least laden with mud, and he
obviously hadn't shaved in days, although admittedly the boy
sported more peach bloom than peach fuzz. The black man
accompanying him was enormous, grizzled, and white-haired,
but impressively muscular.

''Oh, you'll be so pleased,'' Amelia effused at Jeffrey.
''Mr. Fargo has most graciously offered us his hospitality.''

Amelia flashed Fargo a brilliant smile, and he felt his ire
rise. He'd been taken, he realized. Fargo was crackling with
anger, but too dangerously riled to say a word. He felt as
though, if he took any action, he would wipe them all out like
a band of renegade Sioux. But Fargo didn't need to do a
thing. Amelia took care of everything.

''Plato,'' she ordered, ''you bring in the trunks. Oh, and
Mr. Fargo desires a bath. Jeffrey, you can help me hang a
curtain.''

Without pause she went to the bed and snatched a folded
wool blanket from the end of the quilted spread. ''Oh, dear,''
she muttered, scanning the room until she spied several nails

pounded into the log wall. Whatever pictures or calendars the nails had supported were long gone, and Amelia's eyes lit.

While Fargo watched, the black man carried in two oversized trunks, several reticules, and numerous boxes. And Amelia and her brother filled his bath, hung a curtain in front of it, helped the black man situate the trunks, moved the table, spread three bedrolls on the floor, and generally brought total disorder to the crowded cabin.

"Plato, you can serve as Mr. Fargo's valet," Amelia said, seizing control of the men as easily as any cavalry officer. "Use Mr. Jeffrey's things," she ordered.

Fargo stared as the black man immediately started taking toilet articles out of one of the trunks, a towel, soap, a brush.

"And you, Jeffrey, you go back and fetch Aphrodite. I know its a tight fit, but she'll be so pleased not to have to sleep in that dreadful tent," Amelia bantered. "But of course, Plato will have to sleep in the wagon. He doesn't seem to mind, though, do you, Plato?"

"No, Miss Amy. I don't mind."

Almost in a trance, Fargo let the big black man direct him to the bathtub. He'd been had, he thought, as he heard the door slam behind Jeffrey Parmeter's retreat. All he wanted was a hot bath and a warm bed. He'd been on the road for ten days, stopping only to rest the horse, not daring to sleep much himself, traveling alone in Indian country.

Without thought, Fargo stripped down and sank into the hot tub, wearily leaning back to ease his aching muscles. But then two huge hands were upon him, and he sat up, rigid. "What in hell are you doing?" he demanded, swinging around to face Plato.

"I'se only soaping your back, sir," the black man answered, looking affronted.

"Goddammit, call your slave off," Fargo shouted.

"But, Mr. Fargo," Amelia said from beyond the curtain, "Plato is merely trying to help."

"I don't need help taking a bath," Fargo growled, rising out of the water like a wrathful Poseidon. "Get him out of here."

"Plato, perhaps you should best leave," Amelia mewed.

The black man came out from behind the curtain and fairly ran out the door, Fargo coming right after him. Slamming the door on Plato's fleeing form, Fargo turned on the woman, bearing down on her until her back was pressed against the log wall. Her full skirts billowed out in front of her, however, stopping Fargo's advance several feet in front of Amelia's quivering body.

Fargo was huge, naked, and tense with anger. The flickering lamplight played across his wet flesh, illuminating bulging sinew and muscle. Amelia's round eyes widened.

Abruptly, Fargo regained his composure, and realized his position. "You've got a way of managing things, haven't you, Miss Parmeter?" he snarled. "But I'm not so easily managed," he warned her, stepping close enough to displace the full skirts. He towered above her, glaring down at her, giving her just enough room to slide out sideways.

Fargo hoped to send Amelia Parmeter fearfully scurrying out into the mud. But she merely stared. Her dark-blue eyes were level with his chest, taking in the crisp black hair and hardened muscle. Her gaze dropped to his pelvis, and her fascination was obvious. Fargo felt himself respond.

Reaching out automatically, Fargo pulled the woman toward him. He felt her stiff petticoats and gathered skirts press into his groin, and his arms tightened around her. She was tiny, fragile, easily enfolded in his embrace. He pressed harder and Amelia collapsed against the wall.

Fargo felt the rough logs scraping his forearm as he wrapped one hand in her hair to pull her head back. He kissed her, and the urgency of it surprised even him. Lifting his head, he glowered down at Amelia. The look in her eyes was startled and bewildered, but she offered no resistance. Yet, with immense effort, Fargo thrust himself away and grabbed up the towel on the bed.

"You've invited too much company for me to enjoy your attentions," he rasped.

Amelia Parmeter only stared, her eyes round with awe, her lips slightly parted, her bosom rising and falling in unsteady rhythm. She watched as Fargo pulled on his pants, buttoned his shirt, and donned his boots. She didn't say a word when he grabbed his coat and went to the door. Stomping out angrily, Fargo almost collided with Jeffrey Parmeter and a slender black girl.

"Mr. Fargo, where are you going?" the boy asked.

"Out," Fargo snapped. But when the boy's face fell, Fargo added, "To see if I can find a drink in this godforsaken hole."

17

"Could I go with you?" the boy questioned eagerly.

Fargo eyed Jeffrey Parmeter. The boy was probably seventeen or eighteen—old enough. Stepping aside to let the young black girl walk inside, Fargo saw Amelia Parmeter still gazing at him through the open door. "Why not?" he answered sardonically as his eyes met Amelia's. "The more the merrier."

The inside of the one-story, false-fronted saloon smelled of fresh raw lumber and damp sawdust. With Jeffrey Parmeter following intrepidly, Fargo made his way to the crowded bar. The tinny sound of an untuned piano rose above a riotous clamor of stomping feet, hoarse voices, and clinking glasses, providing dubious music as the customers took their turns dancing with the bar girls. There were only three women among the dozens of men, but women were still rare enough in Denver for one to draw an audience.

One of the women slipped away from her admirers and approached Fargo, and the Trailsman almost laughed out loud at the flushed look of awe on Parmeter's face. The boy looked a lot like his sister, though. Suddenly, Fargo scowled.

"What's the matter, cowboy?" the woman asked.

Fargo turned to her, not liking the label she had chosen to give him, although he knew the woman had only called him cowboy because he wore a western hat and tight denim jeans, unlike the miners who almost invariably chose heavier, baggier trousers, more suitable for their work.

"Everything," he answered succinctly.

"Maybe I could make it better," she offered huskily.

"Maybe. Have you got a bed and a private room?" Fargo asked. He heard Jeffrey Parmeter choke on his drink, but he ignored it.

"Right this way," she answered, turning.

"How much for the whole night?" Fargo questioned, holding back.

"You must have been on the trail a long time, mister." She laughed.

"I want to sleep in the bed, not screw," Fargo told her, and Jeffrey Parmeter gagged. "Goddammit, would you be careful?" Fargo muttered, slapping the boy on the back.

"But, Mr. Fargo," he rasped, "you can't talk that way to a lady. She's, she's . . ." The boy spluttered into incoherence.

"Shit," Fargo muttered.

And the woman giggled hysterically. She was the only remotely pretty one of the three dance-hall girls. Probably not quite thirty, plump but shapely, red-haired, with full breasts bulging from her red satin and black lace costume, she was attractive in a brassy way. But her hair was freshened with henna and the coppery color clashed badly with the red dress. And her skin looked too pale, almost sickly, in contrast to the black lace.

But she wasn't bad, Fargo thought. She was actually kind of pretty, discounting the unflattering outfit. Fargo glanced down at her overflowing bodice and smiled for the first time. "Well, mostly sleep," he conceded, taking her arm and leading her away.

Jeffrey Parmeter stayed behind, enviously gaping.

Fargo was tired. He lay on the woman's bed watching languidly as she shed her clothing. Her body was generous and fleshy, but not overblown. Her belly was rounded, her hips full, her breasts large but piquantly topped by small, rouged nipples. She smiled knowingly as she lay on the bed beside him and began to remove his clothing. As she unfastened Fargo's belt buckle, he stared into her cleavage. It was deep and dark. She looked soft, and that was what he wanted, a warm soft place to lay his head.

Fargo's organ responded when the woman pulled his pants free and touched him, but he was almost too tired to care. He sat up to help her with his pants, sinking back without complaint when she got up to fetch soap and water. Following a custom perhaps as old as her profession, the woman washed his organ. And Fargo watched her face.

A small furrow of concentration touched her brow. The water was warm, her fingers were slippery, her eyes were luminous green, her mouth was ruby red. But her eyes were a bit too knowing, a bit too harsh, and her skin, framed by a brilliant cloud of auburn hair, was far too pale, as if it had never been exposed to the light of day. She smiled.

"I guess I pass inspection," he mused.

"Sure do," she agreed. "You can go right to the head of the class."

Turning on his side to watch her plump bouncing bottom as she walked over to the dresser, Fargo laughed at the familiar words, but he didn't feel any undue impatience as she put away her bowl and cloth.

"You look all done in, cowboy," she commented. "Well, not quite," she amended, leaning over to glide her fingers down his turgid organ.

The woman moved around behind him and began to rub his back. Her fingers kneaded at his sore shoulder muscles, traveling up to ease the tension in his neck. Fargo slipped onto his stomach, harboring a vision of toppling the woman down and driving himself inside of her, but he was altogether too content to bother.

"I'm afraid I didn't catch your name," he murmured.

"Clara," she answered. "I didn't catch yours neither," she mumbled. "But then again, most of my friends don't have one."

"The name's Fargo," he offered. "Skye Fargo."

"I've heard of you."

"Good or bad?" he asked.

"Mostly good," she admitted. "But it don't matter none. I know a good thing when I see it."

Smiling, Fargo rolled onto his back, and Clara straddled him. Instinctively, he burrowed his organ into her moist heat. Clara's cheeks flushed as Fargo entered her. Her hips rotated and her eyes glinted beneath her half-closed lids. She was getting prettier by the minute, and Fargo completely forgot that all he had wanted that evening was a bed and a bath.

Clara collapsed on top of him, her billowing breasts pressing into his chest, her fleshy thighs straining against his hard muscles, her hips undulating rhythmically, and Fargo's hands reached out automatically to grasp her buttocks and tighten their bond. The bed was soft, the woman even softer, but Clara wasn't the kind of entertainment a man could sleep through. She rose up over Fargo, tossing her head back and gritting her teeth. Clara moaned. "Please," she pleaded, and Fargo obliged instantaneously.

Grasping her shoulders, he toppled her onto the bed. Following closely, he thrust into her again, pausing to let her catch her breath. But Clara was consumed. Although Fargo blanketed her like a sheet, she struggled to get closer.

She twisted sideways, pressing one fleshy thigh into his pelvis. She twisted again, shoving her belly against his hard muscle before embracing him with both legs to bring him in deeper. She pressed hard with her legs, surrounding him like a rigid steel band, but her hips writhed and rolled. Snaking like a sidewinder, Clara gyrated beneath him. Then, bringing her feet down to plant them on both sides of Fargo, she threw her head back, braced her shoulders against the mattress, and bent nearly double, lifting them both off the bed.

Amazed, Fargo realized that in spite of all her softness, Clara rode like a wild mustang. It took a good man to master a mount like her, but he knew he was just the man to do it. Laughing, he pulled back and came down hard, his muscles grinding into her soft flesh.

Fargo plunged into her, forcing her back down, but Clara pushed back. His weight was superior, but she fought it. She lurched. She pitched. She threw herself against him.

They were slippery with perspiration, and frothing and foaming with movement. There was no taming of Clara. She was a force of nature, and together they were as turbulent and churning as river rapids.

Clara bucked, surged, and heaved, nearly tossing him off, but he held steady. She made noise like a growling animal, and together they set the bedsprings to squeaking with the constant whine of a rusty buggy. Trying to throw Fargo off and hold him close at the same time, Clara gasped and snorted like an angry bull. Then she groaned, and the sound built like a mounting wave, cascading from her like the roaring thunder of white water.

Pressing his thumbs into her hips, Fargo dug his fingers into her buttocks, seeking to imprison her, to hold her still as he rammed into her, driving her hard. But still Clara writhed. Determined, Fargo grasped her hips, holding her down as he slammed into her repeatedly.

Immobilized, Clara strained to keep him inside with her muscles. She squeezed tightly and her muscles quivered. Her thighs held Fargo's slim hips like a vise. Her throbbing muscles surrounded him, and her body pulsated, until Fargo released his hold on her hips, gripped Clara's shoulders, pulled back, and catapulted into her one last time.

Her body shivered, tensed, then seized. And her muscles constricted, pulling the life force from him. Clara screamed, and Fargo dropped onto her chest, pressing his face to her hair. She smelled of sweat and musk, his and her own. And he was tired again, pleasantly, thoroughly exhausted.

"You O.K.?" he mumbled.

"Better," she whispered. "Much better than I been in a long time."

Fargo smiled, thinking that if a man kept a woman like Clara feeling better steadily, he wouldn't last too long. Pulling the bedspread up over them, he stretched lazily, reflecting that it wouldn't be a bad way to go—working every bit of flesh and muscle till it just wore away. Drifting off with one arm slung around Clara's soft shoulders, he was just managing to conjure an erotic image of his own demise when the dream shattered.

A crash sounded in the room, Clara screamed, and a spray of glass rained across them. Instantly, Fargo was wide awake. He pulled Clara over on top of him and rolled, right off the side of the bed. Fargo landed flat on his back. The hard wood jolted him, and Clara's breasts pressed against his face like a smothering pillow.

Fargo pushed Clara away and shrugged out of the entangling bedspread as he grabbed for the gun he had left on the chair beside the bed. "Keep down," he shouted at Clara as he pulled the Colt from his gun belt. Fargo turned and dived under the bed, grimacing as splinters from the rough flooring bit into his arms and knees. But he was very careful not to let his pelvis drop.

Inching forward, Fargo saw the man who had destroyed his peace. The man was on hands and knees, still crouching after his flying leap through the window. Fargo thrust his head out from under the bed just as the intruder got to his feet. Before the man could react to Fargo's motion, the Trailsman brought his Colt around and up. Gunfire exploded in the room. The intruder's weapon clattered onto the floor, and his corpse followed, slowly, anticlimactically, making a hollow, thumping sound as it hit.

Before he could quite figure out what had happened, Fargo was standing over the man, staring down at a strange face. The crimson stain on the stranger's chest looked too small to have caused so much damage, but the man was definitely dead when Clara crept up beside Fargo. Fargo glanced at her, and she catapulted into his arms. Clasping her with one arm, he reached back with his other to set the Colt on the bedside table.

"A friend of yours?" he asked.

"No," Clara sobbed, shaking her head against Fargo's shoulder. Clutching at him, she drew great heaving breaths, and her breasts moved against his chest. "I never seen him before," she whimpered. "You sure he ain't a friend of yours?"

"Pretty sure," Fargo muttered. "I suppose he might have known me, or of me. But I didn't know him. And I sure wouldn't have counted him a friend."

Fargo brought his fingers up and tilted Clara's chin back. "You all right?" he asked.

"No," she denied. Her pale skin was tearstained and her green eyes were wet and sparkling. All the knowing coarseness had drained from her face, and she was just a woman in need of comfort.

It had all happened too fast, leaving Fargo as edgy and sensitive as a bristling cat. He could feel the skin prickle across his bare back and shoulders. And he wanted to pummel the bastard who had, for no known reason, robbed him of his well-deserved lethargy. After ten days of hard riding and little sleep, Fargo was brimming with roiling, seething anger. He was fairly shaking with the urge to wring an apology out of the stranger, but a civilized man didn't go around mutilating dead bodies—even if the stinking bastard did still owe him an explanation. Unconsciously, Fargo tightened his hold on Clara.

He felt Clara's soft rounded belly press against his groin, while her clutching fingers groped frantically at his shoulders. A shock of cold air rushed through the newly broken window, setting the woman in his arms to shivering. Turning Clara away from the window, Fargo reached out to push the curtain over the shattered glass. He scanned the darkness as he did so, but there was nothing moving in the lot behind that backroom of the frenzied dance hall. The tinny music straining from beyond the hallway was all Fargo could hear.

Knowing Clara was much more shaken than he himself had been in many years, Fargo soothed her bare back and shoulders. "Ready to face the law?" he murmured.

Clara trembled. "Give me a little time," she pleaded. "Just a little time. Just stay with me for a few minutes."

Fargo agreed readily. While Clara sat on the bed, he moved around it. He pulled on his pants, then leaned over to fetch the heavy bedspread for Clara, but before he could hand

23

it to her he was lunging across the bed for the Colt. He grabbed it, shoved himself back off the bed, and landed on his feet with the weapon steady in his hand just as the door swung open and Jeffrey Parmeter stepped into the room.

"I thought I heard a shot," the boy exclaimed. "I wasn't sure. It was so noisy in there, but . . ." The boy stopped and gawked, color spreading from his cheeks to the roots of his light-blond hair.

Clara was trying frantically to escape without taking her eyes off the intruder. Scrambling like an awkward crab, she was trying to move backward propelled by her elbows and feet, with her knees up and her thighs spread, revealing flesh still damp from her earlier lovemaking. Abruptly, Jeffrey Parmeter seemed to be in a trance. He didn't even notice when Fargo walked between him and Clara's open thighs. Clara pulled her knees together, and Jeffrey stared at her breasts.

Tossing Clara the bedspread, Fargo rolled his eyes in amusement. "You seem to have a fan," he muttered to Clara.

But the sound of Fargo's voice made Jeffrey recall his manners. He looked away, drawing up shortly and gasping as his gaze fell on the intruder's body. "Why, you've shot Mr. Caldwell," the boy whispered.

Fargo glanced up sharply, dropping his hands from the gun belt he was fastening. "You know him?" he demanded, striding back around the bed to join Parmeter.

"Uh huh." The boy nodded dazedly.

"Why? Where? How? How do you know him?" Fargo questioned.

Jeffrey looked at Fargo with glazed eyes. "I met him," he answered tonelessly, "at Dexeter Plantation."

"What's that?" Fargo demanded. "What's Dexeter Plantation?"

"It's a home," Jeffrey answered. "It's Stephen Dexeter's home. He's engaged to marry my sister." Jeffrey swallowed as he glanced back at Caldwell's body. "As a matter of fact, Stephen came out here with him." Jeffrey's voice was flat and hollow, echoing his shock. "Stephen is a painter. He came out here to do a portfolio on Indians, an update on Catlin's work."

"So why was Caldwell trying to shoot me?"

"Shoot you?" Jeffrey repeated, turning his bewildered gaze on Fargo. "I'm sure I don't know, sir."

"In that case, it seems I've got some more questions to ask, somewhere," Fargo ground out harshly. Sitting down to pull on his boots, he turned to Clara. "I'm afraid you're going to have to face the law without me. Tell the sheriff I'll see him in the morning. If the sheriff's heard of me, I don't think he'll make too much of a fuss."

"You'll come see me again some time, won't you?" Clara whispered.

Fargo's smile sparkled in his eyes. "It will be a pleasure," he told her.

Before leaving, Fargo paused to speak to Jeffrey Parmeter. "I think you'd better stay and tell the sheriff what you told me. And as for Clara, I don't think she should be alone tonight. You'll stay with her, won't you?"

Clara had scooted up on the bed, covering herself, but her rounded, ample flesh jutted out from both sides of the sheet she clasped between her breasts.

Staring at her with lustful intensity, Jeffrey Parmeter swallowed hard. "It will be an honor, sir," he told Fargo.

# 2

Fargo waded his way through the streets of Auraria and Denver, settlements that seemed to offer everything from mudholes and puddles to lakes and swamps. Since no one was particularly fastidious about these burgeoning cities as yet, being too busy building them, the muck smelled of horse manure and rotting garbage. And the air was thick, a choking, hellish swirl of smoke, made even more unpleasant now that the intermittent drizzle had turned to snow.

Some old-timers—trappers and the like—claimed it was an impossible place to put a city. When the winds were wrong, the wall of mountains to the west kept the smoke from going anywhere, and the whole valley got like the inside of a tepee. The Indians had had the same problem. And yet everyone from the Arapaho to the prospectors seemed to gather at that same place on the banks of Cherry Creek.

It was said to have a grand climate, but as Fargo tried to make his way back to his cabin in the dark, he would have disputed the point—although he knew the weather was just another facet of springtime in the Rockies. The rain, sleet, and snow of spring were just ornery companions for the seasonal rock slides and avalanches. After having spent a good many springs in various places from Santa Fe to northern Montana, Fargo wondered why he never remembered the foibles of the season in time to head for Texas.

Fargo heard the approach of a rider behind him, and he moved aside. He was walking down the middle of the street because it was the driest place available. Uptown, if it could be called that, there were a few board sidewalks, and where they ended, the merchants had thrown planks across the puddles in an effort to be hospitable. But out here among the cabins and shanties there was nothing but mud.

"Shit," Fargo cursed as slime oozed over the top of his

boots. Turning, he glared at the rider who happened to be the direct cause of his misfortunes.

For the most part, the night was dark, eerie, dripping wet, uncomfortable, and strangely accented by distant patches of white where the snow was landing on something other than mud. Except in the business sections, there were few real glass windows in the new twin cities. So there was little light in the streets, just hazy patches of lantern glow filtering through windows covered in oilcloth and hides. The approaching horseman was nothing more than a large shadow and the sound of a plodding horse, its hooves splashing in muck.

But something warned the Trailsman, some instinct, and he tensed. He hadn't seen a flash of metal, he hadn't heard anything unusual, but something, some telltale movement or the general outline of the rider, made him sure. He ran around the corner of the closest cabin just as the gunshot exploded. He kept running. The mud crept up around his knees and sucked at his boots; he was fairly swimming in it and barely making any progress.

"Goddamn shit," he muttered as he heard the horseman round the corner and ride into the narrow yard between the cabins. But the horse didn't like the mud any more than Fargo did. It neighed, pawed, and snorted, and Fargo could tell by the rider's oaths that the horse was trying to turn back to the street.

Leaning low, Fargo sloshed through the mud. A bullet whizzed over his head, but he was in the shadow of the cabin and he knew his attacker couldn't see him. Ducking a second shot sent him sprawling facefirst in the mud, but he was up immediately, unhurt and wallowing forward as fast as possible. The man was shooting blind and his horse wasn't helping him.

Fargo reached for his Colt, but his entire body was caked in goop. The Colt was downright slippery and his hands were slick, too. He wiped his palms against his pants as he ran, but it felt as though his whole body had been immersed in axle grease.

The only way the Colt could do him any good was if he had a dry kerchief to wipe it with, and nothing within reach was dry. Reluctantly, he gave up on the idea of stopping to face his adversary, even though losing the option of turning and trying to bring down his pursuer angered him. He couldn't risk losing the Colt. Nor was he sure that the gun wasn't too wet to fire. Another shot from the gunman hit the shanty, throwing a chip sideways to lance Fargo's cheek.

The ground behind the cabin was a little less boggy, and Fargo sprinted from the shadow of the cabin to the shadow of the outhouse. The horse was still coming, but it wasn't making good time. With the outhouse protecting his back, Fargo headed for the sorry-looking plank fence of one of the shanties facing the next street where there seemed to be more lit cabins. Fargo didn't like the extra light, but there was no heading back.

He figured his chances of eluding the gunman were at least even, or maybe good—if a few people would come out and investigate the noise. That wasn't likely, though, since gunfire wasn't exactly rare in Denver. Like most good Westerners, the citizens believed in letting their neighbors mind their own business, especially if that business were something they could get hit by.

His feet weighted with mud—his whole body was covered with the stuff—Fargo felt heavy, but he managed to vault the fence. A low growl greeted him and Fargo froze.

"Goddamn, double shit, damn," he spat as the growling grew more ominous.

He turned slowly to face the dog. It wasn't so light out that he could tell its breed, but he could tell that it was godawful big.

Launching himself forward, Fargo ran straight at the over-sized hound, which turned tail and ran. Fargo veered, and it took a moment for the dog to catch on. But before the Trailsman got anywhere near the fence at the other end of the property, the dog was at his heels, barking in outrage for having been fooled. Fargo pumped harder. His chest was heaving. His legs ached.

If the dog hadn't been at his tail, Fargo wasn't sure he would have made it any farther. But instead of floundering, he reached the fence and nearly sailed over it. On the safe side, he paused to catch his breath and listen. The rider still came but had fallen behind. Fargo didn't feel like thanking the dog for helping him. He dashed for the street.

He knew the rider would skirt the fenced yard on the right. Because a lantern burned behind a hide-covered window, it was brighter over there. So Fargo turned left.

A row of tiny shanties leaned out over the street. There was too much light, a bourbon-colored haze, and Fargo's fleeing figure was a clear target, the only thing moving in the street. Behind him the gunman's horse screeched wildly. It still had to be in the side yard where the unpacked earth could easily reach up and swallow its fetlocks. But once the horse was back out in the street, the mud, only ankle-deep, would barely impair its pursuit.

The awkward weight of mud slowed Fargo's progress, and the damp, frigid air seemed to freeze his lungs. His only hope was to disappear before the gunman saw him.

The gaps between the shanties were too dark and narrow for a horse. But just in case his assailant decided to dismount and search, Fargo dashed past the first shanty, and the second and the third. Then the shrill complaints of the horse lessened, and he dived for cover.

The earth was smothering, fetid, and clammy. Fargo slid on his belly in muck, and the stuff rose up and submerged him. For a moment, he felt as though he were being buried alive, but then he pushed himself up and gasped for air.

Finally, Fargo managed to sit up and lean his head back against the shanty wall. His teeth beat in a staccato chatter and he shivered. Although he drew his knees up close to his chest, there was little body warmth left under his marshy glaze. If he stayed in hiding too long, he just might freeze to death and save the gunman a bullet.

He stood. His feet were still planted in eight inches of muck, but he pushed great globs of it from his body and pulled it from his hair. Leaning far forward, he braced his hips against the wall and rocked back and forth, flexing his knees and hugging himself, trying to keep his circulation going.

Gingerly, Fargo took the Colt from his gun belt. Since the mud was drying already, his fingers were no longer slippery, but they were numb, and the gun was covered with crud. He pushed dirt away from the trigger mechanism, but the barrel was jammed. Angrily thrusting the weapon back into his gun belt, Fargo bent and retrieved his throwing knife from his boot.

He heard the horse go by, the splashing hooves pausing at every gap between the shanties. But it was black in the narrow alleyways, and he knew the gunman couldn't see him.

The horse circled and made it way back up the street. At the end of the row of shacks, the gunman stopped. He was waiting, waiting for Fargo to do something stupid and desperate. He was betting on a hunch that Fargo's weapon would be too wet to fire.

Fargo heard the sound of a horse coming down the next street over, and for a moment he thought of fleeing back the way he had come, but he decided against it. He was too damn cold and stiff to run well, and he couldn't afford to be caught out in the open. Besides, he thought, his attacker might give up soon. His horse was snuffling and nervous. Occasionally, it let out a strange shrieking whinny, the kind of sound that warned a man he wasn't atop a trustworthy mount.

The gunman was hunting him as if he were a small, defenseless animal. Fargo was tired, cold, wet, and miserable, but he was no rabbit. As he bided his time, Fargo let his anger rise, warming him. Slowly it spread out to include Caldwell, the weather, the mud, the city, and finally Amelia Parmeter. If it hadn't been for her, he never would have left his bed that night. And somehow she was connected with all of it.

Caldwell had shot at him earlier, and now someone else was after him. Fargo had his share of enemies, but he was seldom attacked by two different men in one night for two different causes. It stood to reason that the second gunman was connected with the first. And Fargo knew the first gunman, Caldwell, was connected with Stephen Dexeter, and Stephen Dexeter was connected with Amelia Parmeter. The gunman might even be Stephen Dexeter, Fargo realized.

"Goddamn her," Fargo cursed lowly. That little bitch had tried to hire him on the pretext she was merely looking for a straying love. Well, he didn't blame this Dexeter fellow for running from Amelia, but there had to be more to it than that. If it were only Dexeter gunning for him, he could understand it, maybe even sympathize with it, but there had already been two gunmen. If it was the last thing she ever did—and it well might be, considering how Fargo felt—Amelia Parmeter was going to tell him why she was looking for Stephen Dexeter.

Earlier, Fargo had surmised Amelia was probably searching for her fiancé because they had quarreled, or because she suspected Stephen Dexeter wasn't planning on returning for the wedding, or maybe she had heard there was another woman. But men didn't go around attempting murder over someone else's little spats. Fargo was going to get Amelia Parmeter to talk if he had to sit on her. Actually, he reflected, smiling and feeling his face crack as if it had turned into a frozen mask, the idea of sitting on Amelia Parmeter wasn't all too unpleasant.

On the other hand, Amelia Parmeter could wait. After she'd gone to all the trouble of stealing his cabin, Fargo was fairly sure she would still be there in the morning. And besides, even if she weren't, she would be pretty easy to find. An overdressed female traveling with two slaves could hardly escape notice.

Bouncing on one knee then the other while he blew on his numb fingers, Fargo turned his mind to his assailant. The man had presumably come after him because he thought Fargo was working for Amelia. So the gunman was probably someone who didn't want Stephen Dexeter found. Or was it Dexeter himself? he wondered. What would be the gunman's next move? His horse was played out. Fargo had heard the animal snorting and stomping and wheezing and snickering whenever the rider had tried to pull up and listen for Fargo. So first, the gunman would be finding a fresh mount.

Hopefully, the man didn't have any generous friends, Fargo thought as he slipped out of his hiding place and headed for the livery stable. The livery was a chance, maybe a slim one, but a chance. Fargo's clothes were stiff, his body was stiff and his hands and feet were numb. It was nearly a mile to the livery stable, and the mud was still ankle-deep and deeper. Forced to keep to the shadows, Fargo shook and cursed and froze. It took him nigh an hour, but when he came within sight of the livery, he saw there was light pouring from a back window, and his hope mounted.

He stepped inside and the warmth of the place nearly knocked him over. It probably wasn't all that warm, but Fargo was nearly frozen. The smell of horse, leather, hay, and manure made it familiar, a pleasant, homey place, a well-kept stable where the gentle odors blended with the sounds of snickering and stirring horses.

"Anyone here?" Fargo called.

"I'm here," a voice answered as its owner opened a door at the back and Fargo blinked at the light. "Come on back."

Fargo hovered in the doorway, leaning against the door

frame feeling as if he had just walked a hundred miles, and every single one of them was clinging to him in the form of dried mud.

A boy of maybe eighteen or nineteen, a tall, slender, good-looking kid with dark skin and eyes but a shock of golden hair, bent over a ledger at the desk in the back office, meticulously making entries.

"I'll be with you in a minute. Been a real busy night and I got to do this afore I forget," the boy said, glancing up. "Good God, mister. What happened to you?" the boy blurted, then glanced away, obviously suppressing laughter. "There's some hot water on the stove. A bowl, a towel, and some soap over there." He gestured without looking at Fargo, but his effort to hide his amusement failed.

The boy laughed outright then, almost choking on his attempt to stop. "Hell, you're worse off than that horse of Smith's," he spouted, shaking his head.

Fargo was already at the stove, taking advantage of the boy's offer. "What horse?" he demanded.

"Hell, you should have seen it, mister. That horse was covered near up to the withers. And mad. Took a bite out of Smith's shoulder the minute he stepped down." The boy shook his head again, disbelievingly. "Folks is always thinking they can take a shortcut in this place, what with the houses and tents facing every which way," the boy commented wryly. "They don't stop and think what all this excavating for foundations does to a town. Hell, what with all that loose dirt, the place is worse than a swamp when it's wet."

"So this happens pretty often?" Fargo muttered, leaning over the bowl to cup water through his hair.

"Yeah," the kid admitted. "But I never seen the like of you and that horse. Most folks turn around when they're knee-deep. They don't try swimming in it."

"This horse? Was that tonight?" Fargo straightened up. His clothing was still covered in dirt, but his hands, face, hair, and arms up to his elbows were clean. It was the best he could do with a bowl.

"Yeah. Smith brought him in about half an hour ago. It's why I ain't caught up," the boy answered, turning back to the ledger.

"This Smith . . . What does he look like?" Fargo questioned, walking to the desk to stand over the boy.

But the boy was gawking up at him, not answering. "Hell, you're Skye Fargo, ain't you?" the boy murmured.

"Yeah," Fargo agreed, startled.

"If that don't beat all." The boy laughed again, rolling his eyes. He was an easy, friendly kid, the kind women liked and most men got along with. "The sheriff was here not ten minutes ago, looking for you," the boy told Fargo. "He was fit to be tied, too. First you run off from a shooting. Then I tell him all Caldwell's friends left town. That's why he come here, to ask about Caldwell's friends."

"You know Caldwell's friends?"

The boy shrugged. "They came about a month ago, from Georgia," he paused, frowning uncertainly. "Or maybe it was one of the Carolinas. Don't really remember," he admitted. "There's sure a whole passel of men coming from most every place." The boy smiled genially as he leaned back and opened the top desk drawer. "Want a cigar?" he offered.

"Oh, hell, why not?" Fargo agreed, sinking tiredly onto a straight-backed chair sideways. The kid might have enough information to keep Fargo all night, even though he had been looking forward to some sleep. Fargo rested his back against the plain board wall.

"I got some whiskey," the boy added, not even waiting for Fargo's reply before he pulled a bottle and some fruit jars out of a bottom drawer. "Now, where was I?" he mused, sitting back and throwing a lean leg across the edge of his desk. He hesitated as he struck a match on the plank floor, holding it out for Fargo.

Fargo was almost too tired to bend forward for a light, but the kid was a talkative ally, and Fargo sure as hell had no intention of insulting him. So Fargo picked up the fruit jar before settling his shoulders back against the wall. A lot of men took it hard if you wouldn't drink with them. And a lot of people, even young ones, closed right up if you acted too busy to pass the time of day with them.

"You was asking about Caldwell's friends," the boy continued. "They come here with four mules and a wagon, boarded the mules here, and took out riding horses."

"They?"

"Smith, Caldwell, and the other man. I don't rightly remember his name, it was kind of peculiar."

"Dexeter?" Fargo guessed.

"No." The boy shook his head. "That wasn't it. The sheriff asked me the same thing, but I didn't have his name nowhere. Smith signed all the papers and took care of the bill. You going after those fellows?" the boy asked. "I hear when it comes to finding folks, you're one hell of a lot better than the law. Not that the law's going to go after them. From what the sheriff said, this thing with Caldwell was pretty cut and dried."

"It was?" Fargo demanded incredulously.

"Hell, you ought to know, you shot him."

"But why?" Fargo blurted, still focused on the words "cut and dried."

The boy hooted, slapping his thigh and laughing riotously. "I thought it was because he shot at you," he chortled. "Don't you know why?"

"I know why I shot him," Fargo spat. "But I want to know why he was shooting at me."

"Hey, don't get mad," the boy protested. "I didn't mean nothing. It's just, well, I like horses and all, but this is usually one boring job. Tonight kind of perked it up a bit. I didn't mean to be laughing at other folk's misfortunes."

"That's O.K.," Fargo apologized, waving his hand as if to clear the air as he took a drink of the cheap raw whiskey. "I didn't mean to get snappish. It's just been a long night."

"Yeah," the boy agreed, sobering. "Kind of sad about Caldwell, too. Imagine a man like him getting killed over Clara. Clara wouldn't give someone like him the time of day. Wouldn't have no need to, neither. Not in a place where a woman can take a day's pay just for dancing with a fellow." The kid grinned and shrugged. "I'm not surprised she took a liking to you, though," he admitted.

The kid's eyes swept across Fargo with cool appraisal. The boy was a little too cocky, even a might insolent as he stretched out in his chair tilting his head back to blow a smoke ring at the ceiling. He was almost as tall as Fargo, but whereas Fargo was big, broad-shouldered, and muscular, the boy was all lank. Watching him, Fargo felt there had probably been a couple of men determined to take this kid down a notch or two, in spite of his amiability.

But from the boy's swaggering posture, Fargo also concluded it couldn't be easily done. Not that Fargo couldn't do it; he knew he could. But he didn't want to. The kid was affable and he liked him. Fargo also thought he might prove to be useful.

"So you think Caldwell tried to shoot me because of the woman?" Fargo asked doubtfully. The thought hadn't even occurred to him, since Clara had denied knowing the dead man.

"That's what his friends said," The kid shook his head and laughed. "Well, they didn't exactly say that. But then, you hadn't shot Caldwell, back then. But they all come in together at about seven or so, wanting to take their wagon out."

The boy scowled, looking slightly puzzled. "I told them it was a damn-fool idea, taking a wagon out in this weather. Best thing that could happen is they'd sink it up to the axle. But they had this real peculiar story about claim jumpers. Said they had to get right on to Idaho Springs." The boy flashed Fargo a mockingly deprecating grin. "Taking a wagon into the mountains in weather like this? Why, hell, there's probably a foot of new snow not twenty miles up the road. They would have made better time if they'd waited. Been more likely to get there, too."

Mentally, Fargo found himself comparing the boy to Jeffrey Parmeter. There was little comparison. Behind this kid's amused cockiness, there was a lot of the hardened, knowing quality he had seen in Clara, although it sat a bit better in the boy. But both Parmeter and this boy were drawlers. Parmeter's speech was classic southern, but this kid sounded a bit like Missouri or southern Illinois. It dawned on Fargo that it might be important to keep his Southerners straight. There were a lot of harsh feelings building in the South, and politics made strange bedfellows. This kid's voice was almost southern, but there was something else in it, a twangy, low flatness.

"Where are you from?" Fargo asked abruptly.

"Here," the boy answered, eyeing Fargo suspiciously. Apparently liking what he saw, the kid smiled again. "Not Denver, mind you," he went on. "It hasn't been around as long as me. But my folks did a little farming and ranching in these parts."

"And you?"

"Oh, I drifted awhile. Been to St. Louis, New Orleans, New York, San Francisco," he answered, studying Fargo quizzically. "But they didn't seem no better nor no worse than here. Just different." The kid regarded Fargo for several seconds, while Fargo just stared back impassively. "Mister, I thought you wanted to know about Caldwell's friends. Why are you so interested in me?"

But Fargo didn't answer the question. "Do you consider yourself a good judge of character?" he asked suddenly.

"No," the boy denied. "For the most part I think folks are stupid, but I like 'em anyway."

But Fargo thought the kid was damn smart. It took a lot of brains to be easygoing like he was, friendly, calm, easy to amuse but not easy to anger.

"You never told me why you think Caldwell tried to shoot me over Clara. Why couldn't he have had another reason?"

"They all come by and turned in their horses, but Caldwell said he had some business to take care of and left. Smith and that man whose name I don't remember started making jokes about what a sap Caldwell was being over some girl at the Columbine. I told the sheriff that, and he figured that's why Caldwell tried to shoot you."

"But Clara didn't recognize Caldwell," Fargo objected.

"Well, his friends said he was being a real ass, that the lady didn't take no notice of Caldwell at all."

"But a woman remembers a man mooning over her, even if she doesn't take official notice."

"Yeah," the kid agreed, staring into the whiskey as he swirled his glass. "I thought it was pretty strange, too. I never seen Caldwell near any saloon."

Fargo leaned forward. "What's your name?" he demanded.

"Tom. Tom MacFadden."

"Do you think it could have been some kind of alibi? Some kind of story? So that whatever happened—and I'm pretty sure they planned on having me killed, not Caldwell—it would look like Caldwell was just another spurned lover?"

Tom narrowed his eyes thoughtfully before sighing. "Yeah, I guess that's the way of it," he admitted ruefully. "I don't like to think men go around plotting like that. But if Caldwell had been giving Clara the eye, she would have mentioned it."

"You know Clara?"

"Yeah."

"You know her well?"

Tom smiled, almost but not quite blushing. The color was missing, but the embarrassment was there. "Yeah, I suppose so. She calls me her tadpole and a whole bunch of other things I don't like, but I guess we're friends. Real good friends. Clara would have told me if Caldwell was giving her the eye. He was kind of intense, and men like him make her real nervous."

"Intense about women?"

"No. No, I never seen him with no women. He was just the kind of man who's always staring at you when your back is turned."

Fargo smiled. "So they came in at about seven, and Caldwell left. When did Smith leave with a horse?"

"Right after. Said he'd forgot something and had to pick it up."

Fargo laughed. "Caldwell, if I don't miss my guess. I'd bet money Smith was going to help Caldwell escape. But when I came out instead . . ."

"You mean there was some connection between that muddy horse and you?" Tom's eyes slipped down the length of Fargo's dirt-encrusted clothing.

"You're quick." Fargo grinned. "So," he resumed, "Smith came back and he and the man whose name you don't remember left in a wagon?"

"The three of them left."

"The three of them?" Fargo blurted.

"Yeah, them and that painter fellow."

"Dexeter?"

"I don't know. They called him Steve."

"How in hell did he get into this?" Fargo shouted.

The boy stared back coldly. "Mr. Fargo," he said levelly, "I don't take kindly to being yelled at."

Fargo laughed. This kid had style. Fargo could even see why Clara liked him, even if he was a tadpole. "I'm sorry." Fargo grinned, holding up his hands in mock surrender.

"But you've had a rotten night," the boy finished for him.

"Well, Caldwell never got a shot off, but his friend Smith got off four, and two of them were too damn close," Fargo confided, unconsciously rubbing his scratched cheek with the back of his hand.

"He shot at you?"

"Yeah, you surprised?"

Tom stared at Fargo thoughtfully. "No."

"You didn't like him?"

"No," Tom answered flatly.

"So what was Stephen Dexeter like?"

Tom smiled. "The painter? I liked him. The rest of them was kind of creepy, always whispering together, too quiet sometimes, southern slave-owner types, kind of bossy if you ask me."

"How did Dexeter fit in?"

"They come out together. I guess Dexeter paid for the whole damn trip because these other fellows knew the country. But they left Steve out at Niwot's camp afore they ever come into Denver. He was doing drawing out there. Showed me some of his sketches."

Fargo nodded, noting that the boy called Dexeter "Steve" as if they'd made fast friends pretty quickly.

"When did Dexeter come by here tonight?" Fargo asked.

"Ten minutes or so after Caldwell and Smith left. That other man left too, but he told me they was expecting a man named Steve to meet them. Told me to say they'd be back."

"And after Dexeter arrived, did he leave?"

"No, he stayed and helped me with the horses."

Fargo leaned back against the wall and closed his eyes as he thought, running through the night's events, putting them in sequence. There had been four men—Caldwell, Smith, No Name, and Dexeter—traveling together from somewhere down South. Two of them, Caldwell and Smith, definitely hadn't wanted Fargo around. Caldwell was dead, but the Trailsman had enough information to make finding Smith easy. Before he found Smith, however, he wanted to know why the man had been shooting at him. Fargo hated the idea that Smith could die in an encounter between them and leave him as confused as he had been all night.

"You ever heard the name Parmeter?" Fargo asked suddenly.

"Ain't that that pretty little filly? The one that was jilted?"

"What do you know about that?" Fargo asked sharply.

"Nothing. Somebody just pointed her out to me and said she was looking for her lost intended. I suppose lots of men are out here more because they're running from something than because they're looking for gold. But I sure couldn't see running from her," Tom asserted. "Leastways, not until after the honeymoon."

"Amelia Parmeter's looking for Stephen Dexeter, her fiancé."

"That painter fellow?" Tom let the front legs of his chair drop back into place as he swung his own legs from the desk. "He sure didn't seem the type to run out on no woman," he commented.

"Why do you say that?"

"I don't know." Tom shrugged. "He was a good-humored sort. I told him what I thought about taking a wagon out, but he just laughed and said he'd come out West for adventure. So I told him I hoped his kind of adventure included sliding off cliffs. And he just said it did sound exciting. He'd hate to miss it. He was a gentle sort, kind of quiet but friendly."

Tom struck another match and relit his spent cigar. He drew on it thoughtfully, watching the smoke curl as he exhaled. "That was an odd thing," he murmured. "Them others was supposed to be here to find gold, but they didn't seem so eager, leastways not till tonight. Said they had a claim, but they stayed around Denver for weeks. And they kept going out to Niwot's camp. They said it was to visit this painter friend of theirs. But them and Steve didn't seem real close."

"This camp. Could I go there?"

"Sure."

"Would the Indians talk to me?"

"No. They're getting kind of wary about white folks. Niwot's a peace chief. He might talk to you, but he'd be real cautious."

"Would he talk to you?"

"Maybe."

"I speak a little Cheyenne. Some sign language. Will it help?"

"Not as much as it used to." Tom smiled pensively. "That's one of the reasons I liked that Dexeter fellow. The Indians took to him. And he liked them. You could see it in his sketches, the women kind of sad-eyed and frightened of a white man, the men looking a bit hostile and wary, but all of them different from one another. You know, just people, like you and me. Most folks don't see that, that some Indians are nice, some are all right, some are kind of hateful, and some are outright bitter and more dangerous than rattlers."

"Could you take me out there day after tomorrow?"

Tom studied Fargo intently, his dark eyes narrow with concentration. "Yeah," he answered finally. "I'll get someone to stand in for me here. You know," he added abruptly. "I been thinking about what that Dexeter fellow said about coming here for adventure. I'm nineteen years old and I don't think I want to work in a livery stable much longer. Maybe I'll learn something from you."

"You really like Dexeter, don't you?" Fargo asked curiously.

"Yeah, I do." The boy grinned. "But I reckon it's too late for me to take up painting."

Fargo recognized the compliment and smiled sheepishly. He wasn't accustomed to setting an example for youths. "Thanks for the whiskey and cigar," he mumbled as he stood up. "You've been a real help."

The boy was young, but he had been on his own for at least four or five years, and it showed, not only in his penchant for whiskey, cigars, and Clara, but in his manner. Although he covered it well with a seemingly loquacious glibness, he was a bit like the Indians he talked about, a bit wary, a bit hostile. And he was no fool.

But it was hard for Fargo to admit that Dexeter might be a nice guy. Stephen Dexeter had been traveling with two men who had tried to kill Fargo that night. And he was engaged to Amelia Parmeter. On the other hand, it might prove that Stephen Dexeter had jilted Miss Amelia Miranda Parmeter, which would have raised him a few points on Fargo's popularity scale.

At the moment, Miss Parmeter was still not one of his favorite people. But as he plodded back toward the cabin through the icy muck, he couldn't help but smile at the thought of facing her again. There were some things about Amelia Parmeter that any man would like.

# 3

As soon as Fargo stepped into his cabin, any friendly feelings he'd harbored toward Amelia Parmeter vanished. Petticoats and dresses were hung everywhere, festooning the place like party streamers. Fargo tossed linen, ruffles, and ribbons to the floor so he could sit at the table and clean the Colt. But he sure didn't feel very comfortable.

With their contents apparently removed for airing and unwrinkling, Amelia's huge trunks sat against the wall, taking up more floor space than they deserved. The young black girl called Aphrodite slept in the only remotely comfortable place left on the floor. Although two bedrolls were laid out, presumably anticipating Fargo and Jeffrey's return, one was crammed in the ten inches of floor space between the table and the wall, and the other one was placed so that it just might accommodate a short five-year-old. As if things weren't unpleasant enough, the fire was dead, the cabin was chilled, Fargo's clothing was stiff, and Amelia Parmeter was in his bed.

Fargo wouldn't have minded sharing a bed with Amelia, but he sure didn't appreciate having her usurp his. Nor did he like having Amelia turn his place into some topsy-turvy version of a dressmaker's shop. Finishing with the Colt, Fargo stood up while the first gray light of dawn seeped through the window.

"Damn," he muttered as folds of velvet and silk reached out to smother him. Irritated, he pushed aside the froth of garments that hung from a rope strung clear across the center of his cabin. For several seconds, he stared at the still-filled tub of used bathwater, and than at the huge kettle atop the cold wood stove.

Bracing himself, Fargo stripped and plunged in. The water was frostier than a mountain stream, and the cold metal tub tormented his shoulders like shards of ice. It was all Fargo could do to stay put long enough to soap off his muck.

Glancing toward the blond hair that cloaked his pillow and trailed across his bed, Fargo decided Amelia looked comfortable. But then, she probably hadn't let the fire go out until after she was in bed. Thoroughly angry and totally resolved, Fargo stomped to the bed and climbed over Amelia to bury himself under the covers.

Halfway hoping Amelia would wake up and be so shocked by his presence that she'd skedaddle all the way back to Georgia or the Carolinas or wherever it was she came from, Fargo waited tensely. But Amelia merely sighed and pressed herself against him, wrapping an arm around him as if he were a soft, harmless teddy bear. Feeling oddly insulted by her negligence, he drifted off to sleep.

A few short hours later, Fargo opened his eyes to the sound of repeated shrill screams. For a moment, the hair swirling around Amelia's nightgown-clad body seemed to be a wind-swept sea of prairie grasses. Still sleep-dazed, he couldn't make any sense out of her shrieking, but finally comprehension dawned and he realized she was screaming about him being in "her bed."

Meanwhile, Amelia pelted him with one of her slippers, then one of his boots. As Fargo sat up, a hairbrush hit him squarely in the jaw. "Your bed?" Fargo shouted, rubbing his jaw. "My bed," he countered, rising from it furious and naked. "My floor," he added, stalking across the room to kick one of the bedrolls aside. "My cabin," he continued, emphasizing his point by tossing down one of the hanging petticoats.

Suddenly silent, Amelia Parmeter stared at Fargo's naked body with round blue eyes while her servant cowered behind her.

"And what's even worse than what you've done to this place," Fargo resumed, drawing himself up indignantly until his naked body seemed to fill the small room. "I don't get any sleep anymore. And I keep getting shot at."

Still holding one of Fargo's boots in her hand, Amelia managed to close her gaping mouth. "I hardly think you can blame me, Mr. Fargo, if you chose to embroil yourself in a dispute over a woman of ill repute." Haughtily, she tossed back her waist-length hair and glared at Fargo defiantly despite his nudity.

"Since it was one of your friends I shot, I think I can take it you're at least involved," Fargo blurted. "Your brother did say Mr. Caldwell was a friend of yours."

"Mr. Caldwell? You shot Mr. Caldwell?"

"Yes," Fargo spat. "And why not? He attacked me when I was in bed. You and your friend Caldwell seem to have a lot in common," Fargo added. "And I think you'd better put that down," he hissed, eyeing the boot Amelia was about to hurl at him. "If you don't want to have more in common."

The boot dropped to the floor as Fargo gave Amelia a cool look of appraisal. "How do you know I shot anybody?" he demanded suspiciously.

"The sheriff came by here last night to inquire about your whereabouts, and he informed me of your escapade," Amelia replied.

Satisfied with her explanation, Fargo turned away to get dressed. It wasn't easy to turn away. Amelia's breasts were full and high, and the rose nipples were easily discernible pressing against her thin nightgown. She was something to look at, even if she was little else but trouble. Quickly, Fargo pulled on his clothes, donning his coat as he headed for the door.

"Wait," Amelia blurted as he started to leave. "Where is my brother?"

"I left him at the Columbine."

"You left my brother in a brothel?"

"The Columbine isn't a brothel," Fargo objected. "It's a dance hall."

"That's not what the sheriff implied," Amelia protested. "You were in a woman's bedroom when you shot poor Mr. Caldwell, were you not, sir?"

"Poor Mr. Caldwell?" Fargo repeated incredulously. That poor man had meant to kill him. Surely the sheriff had told Amelia that much.

"You didn't answer my question, Mr. Fargo," Amelia persisted coolly, barely wavering as Fargo's gaze bored down on her arrogantly thrust-out bosom. "But you needn't," she continued, glaring at him disapprovingly. "For surely you cannot deny what manner of place the Columbine is, especially after the sheriff revealed you were clearly not only disarmed but totally disrobed when that sordid little melee took place last night. Perhaps the circumstances do, as the sheriff said, protect you from a charge of murder, sir. But certainly you can't think I don't know what you were doing there.''

"No, ma'am," Fargo answered, suddenly smiling. "I'm sure you know all about what I was doing. Maybe sometime we can do it together.''

"Why, you insufferable, boorish . . . Mr. Fargo, you go get my brother, immediately.''

"And spoil his fun? No way, honey. You want him—you get him. I left him in a backroom of the Columbine, last door left. If you get lost, ask for Clara.''

"Damn you, Mr. Fargo," Amelia shouted as Fargo opened the door. "I need to see my brother at once, and you know I cannot go to that . . . that whorehouse.''

Fargo laughed. "I told you, honey. It is not a brothel. It's a dance hall. The women there are paid to dance. They sleep with whoever they want.''

"You can't just leave here," Amelia ranted as Fargo started to shut the door.

"You're going to miss me? Don't worry, I'll be back," he called as he went outside.

Amelia rushed out the door behind him, and stood on the stoop, not seeming to notice the cold, nor that she, a lady, was standing outside with almost nothing on. "Damn you, sir. May the devil carry you to perdition and further," she screamed, but Fargo just kept walking.

Furious, Amelia skipped off the porch and ran after him. Her bare feet slipped in the icy ooze of the yard and she lurched against him, barely managing to stay upright by clinging to his arm. Astounded by her persistence, Fargo stared down at her.

Since the bright sunlight bored through her gown so well that the color of her skin showed through, Fargo figured the cold air couldn't be hampered much by the flimsy garment. She had to be freezing, but she was so damned used to getting her own way, she went crazy when she didn't. Considerately, he held her up.

"Honey, if I'd known you wanted me so much, I would have done something about it last night in bed," he drawled.

When Amelia's arm drew back, Fargo let go of her, stepping sideways to avoid the fist aimed at his chin. With Fargo out of range, Amelia's follow-through sent her lurching forward, but she managed to get her arms in front of her and at least landed on her hands and knees in the mud. "Damn you, Mr. Fargo," she muttered. "Damn you, damn you, damn you."

"Now, is that any way for a lady to talk?" Fargo asked, leaning down to offer Amelia his hand. She eyed his hand contemptuously, but she took it. "But then you're hardly a lady, are you, honey?" Fargo continued levelly. "A well-bred lady doesn't ask the kind of questions you do. So let's get this straight. You want to know what I was doing at that dance hall last night, I'll show you. But if you don't really want to know, I think you'd better mind your own business."

"But it is my business," Amelia mumbled miserably. "You left my brother at that place where a man was killed last night. And over what, sir? Over a disreputable harlot. You left my brother with that woman."

Fargo was amazed. Amelia sounded genuinely concerned. "But Caldwell wasn't killed over Clara," Fargo protested.

"Then who?" Amelia whispered.

Fargo shrugged. "You, I guess."

"Me?"

"He was traveling with your fiancé, Stephen Dexeter."

"But Stephen barely knows Mr. Caldwell," she murmured. "He was merely a man who knew this country, a traveling companion."

"Are you sure of that?" Fargo snapped.

"Yes," she whispered. "We met him together at the Averys'. Stephen only met with him once or twice more before they left." Amelia was no longer ranting. Splattered with mud and shivering, she was bedraggled and seemed confused. And her lips were turning almost as blue as her eyes.

Amelia looked around in bewilderment, apparently surprised to find herself outdoors in her bare feet and nightgown. She blanched as her eyes settled on a wagon whose three occupants were leering as they rode by. "Mr. Fargo, do you truly believe Mr. Caldwell's death had something to do with me?" she asked plaintively.

"I'd never seen Caldwell before, and neither had Clara.

45

Besides, somebody else shot at me later that night, somebody who I happen to know was a friend of Caldwell.''

"I don't understand,'' Amelia whispered.

It was hard to doubt her veracity when she was muddy, shaking, and looked thoroughly beaten, but they hadn't hit it off so well that Fargo trusted her. "Maybe if you'd tell me why you're looking for Stephen Dexeter, it would help. Why didn't you just stay home and wait for him?''

Amelia stared at Fargo, turning so pale he thought maybe she was really freezing to death. He put an arm around her and led her back to the cabin. "Aphrodite,'' he ordered as he pushed the door open, "take care of her.''

Fargo knew damned well he should question Amelia right then and there, before she had time to dry off and get uppity again. But somehow that seemed unfair.

"Good God,'' he muttered distastefully as he stalked toward the sheriff's office. "I just may be turning into a gentleman.''

The sheriff proved to be no help. He was convinced that Caldwell had been acting entirely under the influence of unrequited love. When Fargo told the sheriff about the second assailant, he was equally unimpressed. "Can't you see, it's unconnected,'' the sheriff objected. "You're a famous man. Lots of men must be out to get you.''

In spite of the sheriff, Fargo managed to collect a great deal of information in an afternoon of inquiry. The Southerners had been a curiosity, and almost everyone in Denver had a story to tell about them. Within fifteen minutes Fargo learned that No Name was actually Julius Arbuthnot.

For the most part, most everyone agreed with Tom MacFadden that Smith, Caldwell, and Arbuthnot had all been cold, arrogant, and standoffish to the core. But even more interesting was the fact that, without any prodding from Fargo, a good many people he interviewed thought there was something fishy about them.

"Claimed to be prospectors,'' one old man mused. "Didn't look like no prospectors I ever seed. Didn't know nothing about panning gold. Claimed to have a stake up Idaho Gulch, but they didn't even know where Idaho Gulch was at. Lessen that's where they's at now. Sure asked enough about it.''

"Doesn't it seem odd to you, Mr. Fargo, that gold-seekers

would spend so much time in an Indian village?'' a woman asked. "Those flea-ridden savages certainly don't have gold."

Fargo came away knowing a lot about Caldwell, Smith, and Arbuthnot, but no one he questioned had ever met Stephen Dexeter. Fargo was pretty pleased with what he'd learned, however, by the time he stopped off to make arrangements with MacFadden to visit the Arapaho camp the next day. He also made arrangements to have MacFadden make sure Jeffrey Parmeter was entertained another night.

One more stop, at the home of Drew Dawson, completed Fargo's plans. The man was as effusive as ever and outrageously excited to have the Trailsman visit his home. Fargo had no trouble at all extracting a promise from Dawson to house Aphrodite for the night. Prejudices being what they were, she'd have to sleep on a cot in the kitchen, but that couldn't be any worse than a bedroll on the cabin floor.

Fargo's cabin, when he arrived, had actually been restored to some kind of order. It was a bit overcrowded, with the huge black man hulking about and the young black woman aflutter, but the petticoats and dresses had been packed away, the bedrolls set aside, and the bathtub emptied and shoved into the corner. But the most startling sight was Amelia Parmeter.

Amelia was leaning over the fat-bellied stove, attempting to cook, but she stood so far away to accommodate her flounced skirts that she couldn't reach the skillet with the spatula she wielded. Amused, Fargo leaned back against the door he'd just shut to watch her progress.

"I would have thought Aphrodite would do that," Fargo commented.

"What?" Amelia jumped, spinning around to face Fargo. "Oh," she murmured as her free hand fluttered to her heart. "I thought it was Plato, slamming in and out again."

"Watch out for your skirts," Fargo ordered.

Amelia dropped the spatula to grab her flowing mint-green flounces away from the hot stove.

Picking the spatula up, Fargo held it out to Amelia, and she offered him a smile as blinding as the sudden glint of the sun off broken glass. "Maybe you should let Aphrodite do that," he muttered gruffly.

"Don't be silly, Mr. Fargo. Aphrodite's a house servant. She doesn't know anything about kitchens."

"And you do?" he demanded.

"No," Amelia admitted, laughing. "But I'm more adventuresome." She gave him a flirtatious sidelong look as she once again tried to turn over the contents of the skillet. For Amelia to even reach the frying pan was barely a possibility, but Fargo didn't offer to help. Instead, he went over to the bed.

Putting his hands behind his head, he stretched out and leaned back against the plank wall. "I've found Aphrodite better quarters for tonight," he announced. "A place where she won't have to sleep on the floor."

"Why, how delightful, Mr. Fargo. I'm sure Aphrodite will be most appreciative," Amelia consented easily, turning toward the young black girl, who now cowered in the corner.

If Amelia was acting as if nothing untoward had happened that morning, Aphrodite certainly wasn't. With a hastily wrapped package of food and several coins pressed into their palms by Amelia, the two servants were out of the cabin as quickly as they could go. Aphrodite and Plato didn't seem to like him much, Fargo reflected wryly.

Fargo had intended to get Amelia Parmeter alone, but he hadn't expected her to be agreeable. He eyed her suspiciously as she bustled around the table. Goddammit, what did she want? he wondered. She already had his cabin. All he had left was a horse and saddle.

"Our meal is ready," Amelia called cheerfully. "Would you open the wine, Mr. Fargo?"

The table was covered in white linen and set with real china and silver. Only the blackened frying pan marred Amelia's predilection for elegance. Gingerly, Fargo picked up the waiting corkscrew, hoping that the instrument would be friendly. He had a feeling that southern gentlemen didn't ever crumble the cork into the bottle. But they probably never drank Taos Lightning from barrels either.

Glancing toward Amelia, Fargo tugged on the skewered cork. To his amazement the cork exploded from the bottle with a feel as satisfying as the recoil of his Colt. Fargo felt a surge of triumph, but was forced to suppress it, realizing Amelia probably didn't even see anything unusual about successfully opening a wine bottle.

"Who's coming for dinner?" Fargo asked, noting the third place setting.

"Jeffrey," Amelia answered. "I sent Plato by that place this afternoon to tell Jeffrey when we would dine. He should have arrived by now."

"He's not coming," Fargo volunteered.

"What?" Amelia demanded, blanching.

"Oh, he's fine," Fargo assured her. "Spending the evening with some friends."

Fargo watched with amused detachment as Amelia attempted a brave smile, but then gave it up and gulped down most of her glass of wine. He was almost relieved to find out Amelia hadn't expected to spend the night alone with him. Fargo didn't trust her when she was throwing boots at him, and he trusted her even less when she tossed smiles his way. The feeling he'd had for the last half-hour or so—that she was about to lower a cannon at him—faded as he realized she hadn't meant to make things easy for him.

"You ever met a man named Julius Arbuthnot?" Fargo asked, trying to change the subject casually.

"Why, no, I've never met Senator Arbuthnot," Amelia answered distractedly.

"Senator?" Fargo demanded.

"Perhaps you meant someone else," Amelia said softly, fixing Fargo with a quizzical stare. "Arbuthnot is quite a common name."

"Tell me about this senator. Do you know what he looks like?" Fargo asked as he poured Amelia another glass of wine.

"He must be nearing sixty," Amelia answered slowly. "Surely you know of him. He was quite an important man several years ago. There was even some talk of him running for president, although I can't say I've heard very much of him since." Amelia paused, studying Fargo for several seconds before she turned her attention back to her wine. "Of course, I can't say as I blame the man for divorcing himself from politics," she sighed. "Considering what kind of men are running these days, that despicable Mr. Douglas and that horrible rail-splitter from Illinois."

"What does Senator Arbuthnot look like?" Fargo persisted. "You ever seen a picture of him?"

"I saw him once," Amelia remembered. "At a ceremony, two or three years ago. He was a little heavyset but marvelously erect. At the time he wore muttonchop whiskers, and he had the most startlingly bushy gray eyebrows. He was really quite distinguished.''

Or pompous, the way the Denverites had seen it. He was obviously the same man. Most had mentioned Arbuthnot's eyebrows, although they had all had a different way of seeing them. A woman had said they grew clear together, making the man seem fierce. Whereas the huge blacksmith thought Arbuthnot looked a bit like a caveman he'd seen in a side-show once. The blacksmith claimed the eyebrows made the man's brow stick out too far.

"You ever met a man named Smith?" Fargo asked.

Amelia dropped her fork and Fargo couldn't say as he blamed her. The food was terrible—potatoes burned on one side and raw on the other, elk reduced to strips of leather.

"Don't be silly, Mr. Fargo," she answered testily. "Certainly I've met men named Smith.''

"Quite the socialite, aren't you, honey?" Fargo commented irritably. "I'm sure you've met lots of men named Smith. But this one's dark-eyed, dark-haired, forty or forty-five, medium-height, husky but not fat, wears a mustache. Ring a bell?''

"No," Amelia answered as she poured herself another glass of wine. "No, I don't think I've met him.'' She tossed down the entire glass, and a glint of defiance lit her eyes. "Mr. Fargo," she addressed him sternly. "I am sorry about taking over your dwelling. And I am sorry for this abomination of a meal. I had every intention of trying to make up for any inconvenience I might have caused you. But surely you cannot just sit there and expect me to prattle on about inconsequential matters, considering the circumstances.''

"The circumstances?" Fargo inquired, with the amusement not quite concealed by his lake-blue gaze.

"Mr. Fargo, you must believe my apology for my behavior this morning is sincere," Amelia pleaded, reaching across the table to touch his hand. "Before I made that ghastly scene, I should have remembered that a man like you, a man justifiably famous in this untamed wilderness, couldn't possibly be acquainted with normal conventions.''

"Are you scared of me or yourself?" Fargo scoffed.

"Why, both, sir," Amelia answered ingenuously. "Surely, you know that even the most respectable of women with the very best of intentions sometimes yield to circumstances.''

Fargo stared at her. Amelia was the wiliest, most devious creature he'd ever encountered, and yet she'd just delivered the most candid admission he'd ever heard from a woman. She stared down at her plate of charcoal-fried food and her cheeks glowed like coals against her suddenly ashen skin. The hand over Fargo's felt very hot.

"Shit," Fargo muttered, thrusting his chair back. "Are you trying to distract me or what?" he huffed as he paced across the room. "To hell with what might or might not happen," he snapped. "I want to know why you're here."

Fargo whirled around to find Amelia sitting on the edge of the bed, looking more forlorn than three lost puppies. He went over to sit near her. "Look, I've been attacked twice and shot at four times," he told her as gently as he could manage. "Don't you think I deserve to know why you're looking for Stephen Dexeter?"

"Of course," Amelia breathed. But then she just sat there, wringing her hands.

"Miss Parmeter," Fargo rasped, recalling her from her reverie.

Amelia glanced up at Fargo with a look so beseeching it would have been hard to refuse if it had glistened in the eyes of a rattlesnake. "Mr. Fargo, can I trust you? Can I really trust you?" she whispered.

Considering his thoughts at the moment, Fargo wished she hadn't asked, but he reassured her regardless.

"I never meant to tell anyone this," she murmured. "If Stephen's parents found out through idle gossip, they'd be absolutely devastated. Oh, Mr. Fargo," Amelia cried, reaching out to clutch his shirtfront in her small hands. She stared up at Fargo with tears streaming down her face. "I don't understand any of this. But you have to believe Stephen couldn't have anything to do with the attempts on your life."

"I will or I won't," Fargo answered simply but somewhat unsteadily as Amelia buried her face against his shoulder. He felt her breasts heave against him. "It depends on what you have to say," Fargo finished a bit too harshly.

Amelia nodded, her chin jutting into his collarbone. "After Stephen left, I suspected . . ." She broke off, gasping for air. "I suspected . . ." she repeated, her words muffled against his shirt. "And I went to Dr. White," she sighed. "And he told me . . . he told me . . ." Amelia began again, launching into an impassioned narrative. Most of her words were lost, whispered as they were into Fargo's pectoral muscles, but he really didn't care what she had to say anymore. Amelia's arms had slipped around to encircle his neck, and her breasts quivered against his chest.

Tilting her head back, Amelia stared up at him. "Oh, Mr. Fargo," she whispered, "I truly do want to help you. But all of this is so personal. I don't know anything about Mr. Caldwell," she whimpered. "You do understand, don't you? You will look for Stephen?"

Fargo didn't make any promises about Stephen. Instead, he did the only thing that seemed natural: he kissed her. Amelia's body stiffened in his arms momentarily, and Fargo braced himself, fairly certain she was going to pull back and slap him. But then Amelia melted against him, and her tongue snaked out to touch the tip of his.

Seemingly oozing like hot wax, Amelia slipped down in Fargo's arms and buried her face against his neck, nibbling upward to nip at his earlobe. "Oh, Mr. Fargo," she moaned, before wilting completely. Amelia fell back onto the bed like a limp little rag doll. Her eyes glittered unnaturally and her cheeks were splotched with high round spots of color.

"You're drunk," Fargo commented, surprised. She'd only had three or four glasses of wine, and he'd thought the stuff tasted as weak as water.

"Oh, yes," she agreed breathily, wriggling sinuously back on the bed. Smiling, Amelia closed her eyes, undulated her shoulders, and looked about as rigid as a piece of rope.

"A gentleman doesn't take advantage of a drunken lady," Fargo said, feeling it was only fair to remind Amelia of what she was supposed to be.

Amelia's eyes flew open and her smile disappeared. "You mean you won't . . ." she gasped.

"Nope," he answered, slipping down beside her. "Didn't mean anything of the sort. I was just telling you about gentlemen."

Amelia shifted sideways, trying to wrap her legs around Fargo, but her attempts only served to bunch her voluminous skirts between them. Her hairpins bit into his hand, and Fargo eased them out, tossing them onto the floor one by one before he tugged her against his chest, moving his hand down to deal with her buttons. It seemed as if there were a thousand of them, a thousand tiny pearl buttons.

Groaning, Fargo fumbled with the buttons, buttons that were obviously meant to be patiently unfastened by a servant under a strong light. While he unfastened her, Fargo pressed his lips to Amelia's, stifling any words that might belie her actions.

Finally freeing Amelia enough to push the mint-green material off her shoulders, he stared down at the swell of her breasts bulging above a lacy ruffle. Pulling back, Fargo took a deep breath and sat up, and Amelia followed his lead. She gazed at him with a hurt, bewildered expression, but Fargo merely grasped her shoulders and turned her around so he could work on her buttons in earnest.

Even when he could see them, the itty-bitty buttons were tricky, with holes sewn so tight it was a bit like threading needles. And he had no sooner gotten them all undone than he realized he still had to deal with her corset. And over that she had on a cotton shift.

"Goddamn," Fargo muttered, sliding his fingers over the layer of cotton covering the tight lacings and curved bone stays of the corset. "It's a prison."

Giggling riotously, Amelia twisted and slipped her arms around his neck. "Oh, Mr. Fargo." She laughed. "You're so funny."

Her laughter had a wine-soaked, bubbly sound that cheered him considerably. "Funny, huh?" He grinned. "So that's what you think," he mocked, ducking his head to flick his tongue across her breasts. He tasted the flesh deep in her cleavage before running his tongue back and forth along the lacy border of her chemise. Amelia's breathing grew fast and thready, punctuated by little sighs.

"Well, back to business," Fargo announced, tugging her sash loose.

"Oh," Amelia sighed dejectedly. But then she bounded from the bed, laughing as she pirouetted in unsteady circles. "I'll help," she suggested, staggering dizzily as she hiked her skirts up and tugged a petticoat down, then another, then another, pausing only to kick them aside. Underneath she wore some kind of lace-layered pantalets that looked to have enough ribbons and bows to furnish a millinery. Hooking her thumbs at her waist, Amelia pushed them down, revealing the first flash of flesh Fargo had seen, and she was still far from naked.

Half-awed, half-appalled by the sheer extravagance of her underwear, Fargo watched Amelia swoop down for the pantalets. Whooping, she twirled them over her head, letting them fly in Fargo's direction. He caught them easily in one hand, then held them up. "Wouldn't these have been enough all by themselves?" he questioned.

Laughing giddily, Amelia came back and dropped beside Fargo on the bed, swinging her legs across his lap while she pulled up her skirts. She began to unroll one of her stockings, finally baring one slender leg.

"It takes a lot of petticoats to replace hoops," she confided. Amelia glanced up at Fargo, and a tiny furrow of worry touched her brow. "Maybe hoops would have been easier," she mused solemnly.

"Well, you can't plan on everything." He shrugged.

"No," Amelia agreed. "I certainly never planned on this." Clasping her arms around Fargo's neck, Amelia leaned back and offered him a dazzling smile, a coquettish smile, the kind Fargo figured she used to make a man move mountains for her, while she didn't so much as take off a glove. Yet Amelia had far more than her gloves off.

"Who would have thought it?" he muttered.

"What, sir?" She laughed.

Fargo felt it best not to tell her that in spite of her self-righteousness, he didn't think the women at the Columbine could be any more obliging than she was being. "Oh." He shrugged, smiling. "I just didn't think I'd ever be glad to see my cabin covered with your petticoats."

Amelia's expression grew dewy and soft. "Kiss me," she murmured.

Fargo was glad to oblige, but Amelia was clinging to him a bit too tightly, and she was gazing at him with something that almost looked like adoration. He began to wonder just how drunk she was—because he sure didn't need to have Amelia Parmeter following him around like a lost pup, especially since it looked like she could afford to hound him for the next ten or so years.

"You aren't taking this too seriously, are you, honey?"

"Seriously? Oh, no," she murmured. "I don't think I could take anything seriously right now."

"Good," Fargo muttered as he rolled down her other stocking. He tickled her toes, laughing with her as she giggled, then slid his fingers up to tease the flesh between her thighs.

Amelia fell back on the bed and tugged her dress up around her hips. Her hair was spread out to either side of her, thick and golden, and her lips looked as red and soft as petals of Indian paintbrush. She wiggled against his hand. "Please," she moaned, grabbing Fargo's other arm to pull him down on top of her.

"Oh, no you don't, honey," he muttered, pulling her back up. "I want to look at all of you." From what Fargo could see, Amelia Parmeter was the kind of sight a man came across twice or thrice in a lifetime, and he wasn't going to miss any of it. Amelia sat facing him and trembling slightly as Fargo slipped her dress down around her waist. "Why don't you take this off?" he suggested, fingering her chemise.

To Fargo's surprise, Amelia got up on her knees and tugged the chemise out from under her dress, then pulled it over her head, before she pulled her dress back up over her corset, modestly holding it in front of her. Her head was down, her eyelids lowered, and her gesture made no sense to him at all.

"Is something wrong?" he asked.

"No," she whispered. "It's just . . . I've never bared my bosom to a gentleman before."

Manfully, Fargo stifled his laughter. "What about the rest of you?" he asked, thinking that for a woman who had just had her skirts hiked up around her waist she was acting damned peculiar.

"Why, of course," she murmured. "You have to bare that in order to . . ." Amelia colored wildly, twisting away from him as if she was about to bolt.

"Hey, sshhhhh, settle down, sweetheart," he soothed, catching her in his arms.

"Maybe we should turn off the lantern," she suggested.

"You are a bundle of contradictions, aren't you?"

"Me?" Amelia asked. "I'm just a little nervous. Maybe I need a little more wine." She glanced toward the table hopefully.

"Maybe you need a little more air," Fargo countered.

"Why don't we take this contraption off?" He slid his fingers along her side, indicating the corset.

"All right." She nodded dazedly, turning her back to him.

Fargo pulled the knotted tie loose, hoping the whole thing would pop apart, but he had no such luck. "I wouldn't have thought you were so fat you'd need all this," he muttered, staring at the maze of ties.

"Fat?" she protested, recovering some of her former exuberance. "I'll have you know I have a nineteen-inch waist, without the corset."

"And with it?" he jeered.

But Amelia didn't seem to notice Fargo found the very idea of her wearing a corset preposterous. "Seventeen, at the most," she stated firmly.

Amelia was laced up like a lumberjack's boot, with the ties knotted here and there to keep them from slipping. But Fargo made pretty good progress, until he came to a tight knot about halfway up. "Damn," he muttered.

"Maybe if I held my breath," Amelia murmured, proceeding to do so. She sat very straight and prim, holding her breath until she swayed.

"Amy, honey, I think you'd better breathe."

Huffing, Amelia leaned her head back against Fargo's shoulder. He could hardly work on the corset with her resting against him, so he put his arms around her and nuzzled her hair. He didn't have much faith in her sanity anymore, but he was actually starting to kind of like her.

"I want to thank you," she murmured.

"Thank me?"

Amelia shook her head, flexing her shoulders as she settled back against Fargo's chest. "It's been so scary," she whispered. "Not being able to talk to anyone at home, then coming out here not knowing what Stephen will say when I see him, of *if* I'll see him. I needed a friend. Just somebody to listen."

Fargo realized he hadn't heard anything she had said. He tried to remember it. Something about a Dr. White telling her something.

Oh, my God, she's pregnant, he thought. Startled, he dropped his arms from around her. Then, automatically, he pressed his hand against her abdomen, but she was still encased in the bone corset.

Aw, shit, Fargo cursed to himself. He sure wasn't going to play the substitute father if Stephen Dexeter didn't want the role, but that was probably exactly what Amelia expected. On the other hand, she had come out looking for Stephen. And it was easy to see why, because it could prove pretty embarrassing to not have Stephen show up for another six or eight months when he had already been away from her for three. So maybe all she wanted was Stephen, and Fargo's help.

"Mr. Fargo," Amelia murmured, turning toward him with a questioning gaze, and she really did look frightened. One thing was certain: she did need a friend.

Fargo took Amelia in his arms, and he heard her sigh against his chest. So he whispered all the things he thought she'd want to hear—that she was beautiful, that everything would turn out all right, that Stephen Dexeter couldn't possibly turn her away. And while he was doing it, he somehow managed to get the corset untied.

There was a furious pounding at the door. "Fargo, open up," Tom MacFadden yelled.

Screeching, Amelia jumped away from Fargo as if she had been stuck with a cattle prod. Desperately, she tried to pull her dress in place over the sagging, untied corset, and she turned pale as she looked down at her scattered petticoats. "Oh, Lord, what have I done? What have I done?"

"Nothing, honey. Nothing at all," Fargo assured her.

"Damn you, Fargo, open up," MacFadden demanded, and Amelia shuddered.

"Wait a minute," Fargo ordered. He scooped up Amelia's underwear and dropped it into one of the trunks, then took Amelia by the waist and directed her into the straight-backed chair.

"How could you have let me do this?" Amelia demanded, turning the chair away from Fargo to emphasize her accusation.

Fargo rolled his eyes. "I wouldn't do that if I were you, honey," he muttered, running his fingers down the exposed curve of her bare spine beyond the chair rungs. "I'd keep my back to the wall."

"Oh," she fumed, turning the chair back around as Fargo answered the door.

MacFadden swept into the room. "You got to come with me," he told Fargo.

57

"Now?" Fargo protested, thinking that he could easily calm Amelia into friendliness—if he didn't leave.

"Now," MacFadden barked, grabbing Fargo and trying to pull the larger man out the door. "Oh, good evening, ma'am," MacFadden muttered, tipping his hat to Amelia, who sat in the chair as rigidly as any spinster. But her hair was loose and tussled, a riotous splendor spilling across her arms and shoulders, plus her cheeks were red, her dress was slack, and MacFadden was no fool.

Fargo balked about leaving only for a moment, knowing MacFadden wouldn't have come if it wasn't important.

Once outside in the brisk night air, Fargo faced Tom in the moonlight, so bright that it cast distinct shadows. "This better be important," he told the stable hand, "or you're in deep shit."

"I ain't the one that's in deep shit. It's Jeffrey, that dimwit brother of hers. And if we don't move fast, he'll be deader than a turd in a milk bucket." MacFadden pointed down the muddy street toward the river. While MacFadden explained Jeffrey's predicament, they trotted that way, their boots sloshing but not sinking more than an inch or two on each step.

As per Fargo's request, Tom had kept Jeffrey out of the way by visiting the Columbine, where they'd indulged in several schooners of Rocky Mountain lager. Fargo recalled it was a vile yellow liquid that would pass for drinkable beer only in a place where nothing else was available. The best that could be said for the local brew was that it was impossible for anyone to drink enough of it to get into trouble.

But something must have gone to Jeffrey's head, because the boy had managed to get himself in a genuine stand-off-at-twenty-paces pistol duel with Powder Pete. Between deep running breaths, MacFadden recounted that Pete had mentioned certain womenflesh that had arrived recently, and he most admired a blond southern belle he took for a high-toned, high-priced whore.

"He didn't say it all that loud," Tom explained, "and he backed off it right away. Pete didn't mean nothin' by it, I'm sure. If it'd been my sister, or even my mother, he was talkin' about, I don't think I'd have felt all that insulted."

Even if Pete had just been thinking out loud, Jeffrey hadn't seen it that way. And MacFadden hadn't been able to talk any sense into Jeffrey because three other cotton-belt gallants had been sitting at their table. "They kept egging him on," MacFadden concluded, "and no matter how much I tried to talk him out of it, Jeffrey is bound and determined to defend his sister's precious honor."

Fargo tried to keep his chuckle to himself, but MacFadden must have overheard it. "I know, if he'd been serious about protecting her virtue, he'd have been at that cabin with the two of you," Tom added as they turned a corner and saw the crowd in the moonlight.

"Best you mind your own business," Fargo told the grinning boy. They paused at the edge of the throng that lined the street, and Fargo took in Jeffrey's predicament.

Toward their end of the block, the young southern gentleman stood tall and proud, his jittery nerves betrayed only by the way his hands kept shaking as he inspected a twinbarreled pistol that had just been handed to him by one of his seconds, the three lads he and Tom had been drinking with.

Down the street, perhaps twenty yards from Jeffrey, stood Powder Pete. Pete was sometimes a bully and always a loudmouth, but unlike most, he could back his bluster with fists and, when necessary, gunplay. Like most men in the region, Powder Pete was no candidate for sainthood, but he was trying to draw the line somewhere short of cold-blooded murder.

Given Pete's experience and Jeffrey's youthful stupidity, though, any duel between them would be just that—murder. For Pete, killing Jeffrey at twenty paces here would be less trouble than swatting a fly on his arm.

Before Fargo could turn to MacFadden, Pete's deep voice boomed out over the murmuring crowd. "See here, Mr. Parmeter, I done told you that I didn't know she was your sister. So let's just say I apologize, I'll buy you a drink, and we'll say no more about it."

Fargo felt a sudden hope that this moonlight gathering might reach a sensible outcome, but that vanished when Jeffrey's thin voice replied, "Never, you despicable cur. You have insulted my beloved sister. You have trampled the proud name of Parmeter. You have besmirched the pure womanhood of the South. I demand satisfaction, you vile wretch." On legs as gangly and unsteady as a fresh-born colt's, Jeffrey began to walk toward Powder Pete.

Pete, short and stocky, sported a luxuriant chest-length

beard, which bristled as he glared at Jeffrey. "Look, you corn-pone whelp, I could eat your liver and lights for breakfast. You got as much chance against me as you would walkin' into a buzz saw. I've killed better men with my eyes shut and one hand tied behind my back. Can't you just give up on this foolish notion? I already said I was sorry."

Jeffrey shook his head defiantly, and the crowd's murmur returned. Fargo heard a man in front of him say, "Twenty to one on Pete. And I'll put up whatever's in my poke—must be a couple ounces anyway." From up and down the street came catcalls: "C'mon, Pete, teach him a lesson." "You're a chickenshit if you back down, Pete." "Let's get this show going."

The Trailsman reckoned there wasn't a lot of formal entertainment in an isolated spot like Denver City, so the men made their own. They gladly watched and wagered on dog-fights, cockfights, and manfights, and everything they bet on was a duel to the death. Considering that the audience consisted of about two hundred men, most of them armed and at least half-drunk, the scene could get even uglier if the onlookers were deprived of the excitement they anticipated. Nothing half so interesting had happened in the three weeks since they'd stoned a Chinaman.

Fargo leaned against Tom and whispered. "Get him the hell out of here when the ruckus starts."

McFadden started to ask, "What ruckus?" but then caught Fargo's meaning and began to elbow his way through the three-deep row of spectators that separated them from the clearing in the middle of the street.

There Jeffrey stood, clasping his pistol, waiting for Powder Pete to arrive so they could stand back to back and settle their argument like gentlemen—or like damned fools. Fargo wasn't sure there was any difference. As soon as MacFadden was on his way, Fargo leaned forward and grabbed the shoulders of the betting man in front of him. Lifting a muddy boot, he planted it on the man's ass and pushed. Just as his powerful leg reached full extension, Fargo released his grip on the man's shoulders, propelling the man's torso forward.

The man's knees jackknifed as he emitted a hoglike whining grunt. He didn't hit the street because another spectator blocked his way. Two more onlookers went down like dominoes before the portly man who had been enjoying a ringside view found himself facedown in the mud with a quarter-ton of wriggling humanity atop him.

A tall, lean rawboned man standing at Fargo's right leaned over to get a better angle on the commotion. The man's lantern jaw was too prominent a target for Fargo to resist, and the Trailsman sent him reeling back with a sharp right uppercut.

The lanky victim windmilled around, staying on his feet while striking at least three folks who hadn't known, until then, that they were in a fight. They started swinging at him, he retaliated, and the brawl spread as their punches, kicks, and lunges landed with careless abandon on bystanders who, if they weren't already involved, quickly joined the melee. They had to get even.

Over on Fargo's left, half a dozen spectators had bunched up to where none of them quite saw him belt the biggest one, a husky roustabout almost as tall as Fargo, with a roundhouse to the ear. The man was too big to fall from the punch, but he was surprised and momentarily stunned. Fargo sidled around behind him and shouldered his way into their huddle.

"Same son of a bitch clipped me, too," the Trailsman announced. "Rat-faced kid in overalls. I was chasin' him when he got you, and then he ran off that way." Fargo motioned toward Powder Pete's end of the street. The knot broke up and six men surged down the block, mayhem on their minds as they grabbed and pushed, looking for the kid in bib overalls. They weren't real polite about it, Fargo noticed, and within the minute, every man on the street was caught up in a general free-for-all of fists and feet that spread like wildfire on the prairie.

Any minute now, Fargo thought, the citizens of Denver City were going to get serious about this moonlight brawl and start working one another over with boards, rocks, knives, and bullets. Noticing a lull in the action right around him, he straightened from his fighting crouch and scanned the scene. MacFadden must have spirited Jeffrey away, probably by cold-cocking him and dragging him off, since neither was visible among the standing or among those who were rising from the mud to rejoin the battle.

The first escape route he had picked upon his arrival, a narrow alley that started between two false-fronted saloons and led uptown toward the cabin, was blocked by two men trading insults and punches to little apparent effect. One took a wide swing and called the other "a worthless weasel from Auraria, that two-bit bunch of shacks with the ugliest whores in the world."

The other responded with a jab and the information that "Any son of a bitch that admits to living in Denver City is nothing more than a back-shooting claim-jumper that don't know shit from wild honey."

Heading on down the street was out of the question if he planned to get home before sunrise, especially if he wanted to arrive without any new scars or fresh bruises. The other side of the block held only three ramshackle buildings, all backed closely against the sandy banks of the South Platte River. Going that way offered precious little cover for someone trying to get away without being noticed, so Fargo turned, determined to go back the way he had come.

He shuffled around eight or ten men gleefully having at one another and stepped easily over the plump legs of a fat man wallowing in the street whose hands slipped out from under him every time he tried to get up on all fours. He ignored several shouts that questioned his manhood and bravery. Rounding the corner, Fargo realized that he wasn't home free yet.

His first impression was that one of the mountains west of town had planted itself in front of him, but the hulk before him was only the same local blacksmith that Fargo had talked to earlier that day. The huge fellow with arms the size of tree limbs had seemed friendly enough then, but now he was eager to join the brawl, and Fargo looked like as good a place as any to start.

Twisting his head, Fargo easily dodged the blacksmith's first clumsy swing while getting in a poke of his own, a left uppercut that drew blood from an unshaven cheek. Fargo had put some muscle into the punch, but it had no more effect than a mosquito bite as the blacksmith lunged forward, trying to get his viselike arms wrapped around Fargo. Fargo began to sidestep, hoping to trip his opponent and get on up the street, but the mud played hell with his footing.

Somewhere there lived snakes, the Trailsman knew, that killed their prey by squeezing it, but he doubted that the snakes enjoyed the process as much as the grinning blacksmith seemed to, and Fargo wasn't enjoying this at all. Fargo was big, but the blacksmith had a good four inches on him in height, and those massive arms manifested the strength acquired by swinging a four-pound hammer all day every day.

Fargo's feet were off the ground as he felt the blast of cheap whiskey odor from the man's breath. Kick and twist as he might, nothing seemed to bother the blacksmith, who seemed as happy as a pig in shit, now that he'd gotten to be part of the brawl that everyone in town would be talking about for the next month or so. Fargo wanted to say something like "Okay, you've had your fun and you made your point. You've got something to brag on now," but he found it impossible to speak as the grip grew ever tighter.

Even breathing was getting to be hard work now, and he wondered how long his ribs could resist getting squashed into jelly. Fargo stiffened and spread his shoulders, gaining a little against the tremendous force that enveloped his trunk. When he felt the pressure increase, Fargo suddenly relaxed.

Before this goliath could tighten his bear hug, Fargo brought up a knee where it would do the most good. The smith's arms dropped, as did Fargo, landing in a crouch, his arms and chest afire with pain. The blacksmith recoiled, eyes now glistening with anger.

"Harm my family jewels, will you?" the smith shouted in the brogue of Ireland as he threw a roundhouse that would have shattered a brick wall. Fargo ducked under it and lunged forward, ramming his head into the man's solar plexus and springing back to get out of arm's reach. Doubled over and gasping, the huge man grasped wildly, trying to get a grip on the source of his pain.

Good blacksmiths, Fargo knew, were hard to come by, and he didn't want to deprive Denver City of one who was a decent-enough guy when sober. But the man was looking for a fight and wouldn't give up as he lumbered toward Fargo. This time, Fargo's footing was solid during his sidestep. His body moved, but one leg remained to trip the blacksmith, who couldn't stay afoot after Fargo's left uppercut caught the tip of his chin and snapped his head back. Like a tree being felled, the blacksmith straightened, tottered, and collapsed.

Looking up the street, Fargo saw his way was now clear, and the noise around the corner had settled to a dull roar. The blacksmith probably wouldn't have anything worse than a headache in the morning, which he wouldn't mind at all because he'd be able to join all the talk about the big brawl.

Fargo judged that nothing inside himself had been broken during the bear hug, but his chest still throbbed with every breath as he carefully made his way to the cabin.

Inside, Jeffrey snored peacefully, his legs draped over the tiny sleeping space Amelia had left for Fargo.

Momentarily wondering why he had gone to all that trouble, Fargo peeled off his muddy clothes, shoved Jeffrey's limbs aside, and crawled inside his bedroll.

# 4

Two hours of the Ovaro's ground-eating trot hadn't done a thing to make Fargo's aching ribs feel better as he and Tom MacFadden rode into Niwot's camp. About fifty tepees were scattered through a cottonwood grove that sat fifteen miles northwest of Denver City.

Judging by what he saw around the camp, Fargo figured most white men he'd encountered lately would enjoy living like the Arapaho. Everywhere he looked, the women, clad in soft deerskin dresses decorated with porcupine quills and trade beads, were doing all the work. Three chattered like jaybirds while they scraped fleshy remnants off a buffalo hide stretched in a wooden frame. Other womenfolk braided hair ropes and bridles, and some were fetching today's lunch. He and Tom had to rein up as a pack of yapping dogs raced in front of them, chased by a pack of eager children and several women who were holding rocks over their heads, ready to brain a puppy and heave it into the stewpot.

A graying dog man, one of the tribal elders, sat before his tepee and greased a bow with rancid bear fat, stopping occasionally to pluck a louse from his scalp and pop it into his nearly toothless mouth. He was the only man in the camp doing anything that remotely resembled honest work. All the others lounged about, smoking clay pipes and swapping lies, their wary brown eyes focused on the two white men who dismounted in the center of the camp.

Fargo knew sign language well enough to get by when he had to communicate with Plains Indians, and he knew the Arapaho language was related to Cheyenne, which he had a smattering of. Nonetheless, he was content to let MacFadden do the talking when they were greeted by a young warrior, clad in a decorated buckskin shirt and woven leggings that extended from under his tanned breechcloth down to his elkhide moccasins.

Most Indians tended to be short and stout, but the Arapaho were lean and taller than most white folks. Niwot—the man's chiefly bearing was unmistakable as he strode toward them— was big even for an Arapaho. Fargo judged Niwot to be almost as tall as himself, although not quite as husky. Going one on one with the chief would be interesting, Fargo thought, but he hoped they were on the same side today.

*"Neisana hinanaeina,"* MacFadden said, raising his right hand in friendship.

Niwot raised his left hand and responded with the proper Arapaho formality. He dropped his hand to his side and smiled at MacFadden. "My heart is glad," he told MacFadden in English, "to hear that my brother has not forgotten how to speak like a human being." Plains lore had it that Niwot was the only southern Arapaho who had learned the white man's speech. Mahom, his older sister, had married a white trader down by Bent's Fort years ago, and the trader had taken a shine to the youngster and tutored him.

Niwot introduced the principal men of the tribe, who seemed reasonable sorts, except for Heap of Whips, a young brave who obviously had no use for Fargo or any other man with blue eyes. MacFadden, in turn, introduced Fargo. "I have heard much of you," the chief responded. "They tell me your medicine is so strong that you never lose the trail when you are following an evil man. It is my hope that no evil man's trail brought you here."

"If evil men have visited here, they have gone," Fargo replied. "We come to our brothers in peace and goodwill." So far, the Arapaho had never bothered him, he had never bothered them, and he wanted to keep it that way.

Fargo wanted to explain that he had just come to ask some questions about the white men who'd been hanging around the camp, but he realized that rushing matters would do no good. Indians ran on a different notion of time than whites did, and it didn't bother a chief one bit to spend six hours of long-winded jawing to accomplish what could have been done in ten minutes of straight talk.

The Trailsman didn't see as he had much choice as they retired to Niwot's tepee. Sitting around the small fire that smoldered on stones in its center, they all leaned back on buffalo-robe pads and smoked a choking mixture of kinnikin-nick, cottonwood shavings, and worm-ridden black plug trade tobacco. As the pipes went around and around, Niwot translated both ways while they discussed the fickle spring weather, the shortage of firewood, the declining population of the southern buffalo herd, and a glorious battle along the Arkansas ten years ago when many Arapaho had counted coup on the bandy-legged Comanches.

This tedious, rambling conversation paused for lunch as a woman brought in an iron kettle. With a forked stick, Niwot reached into the steaming kettle and pulled out a chunk of stringy meat and laid it on the fireside stones as a burnt offering. Another speared piece was held above it as Niwot intoned to the Man Above before lowering the stick toward the ground so that he could ask Mother Earth for strength.

Fargo's stomach felt queasy enough from all they'd been smoking, but he didn't dare offend his host. He took just enough of a helping to be polite and tried to ignore the sound of dogs yapping outside.

Eventually, their talk got around to the four recent visitors to the Arapaho camp. Niwot spoke fondly of Dexeter. "When he learned that my name means Left Hand in our tongue, he said his name meant Right Hand in the tongue of your Latin tribe, and that the two hands should work together in harmony." Niwot passed around a buffalo hide, tanned to resemble parchment, upon which Dexeter had sketched in charcoal. Fargo saw that the artist knew his business. It was a broad panorama of the camp, and small as the human figures were, he could recognize distinct faces, including some of those sitting across from him.

Dexeter had stayed with the Arapaho for the better part of a month, but the three men with him—Smith, Arbuthnot, and Caldwell—had come and gone with their wagon. First they had given Niwot's band sugar, flour, and coffee. "They made great promises that they would give us more," Niwot explained, "if our people would make war on the White Eyes—ride against his camps, burn his farms, drive off his cattle, and take his women."

"Did they say why?" Fargo asked, keeping a poker face to avoid betraying his eagerness.

Niwot leaned back. "They said it would help in a war they plan against the Blue Sleeves. And if we would help them win their great battle to keep the Blue Sleeves from stealing their slaves, then my people would always have full bellies.''

"It sounds like a good deal for your people," Fargo replied, hoping to provoke further comment from Niwot. But it was Heap of Whips who started jabbering excitedly, pointing toward MacFadden and Fargo with hostile gestures.

Once the outburst subsided, Niwot spoke. "Forgive my brother Heap of Whips. He says that no promise from the White Eyes ever means anything more than a fart let loose in the wind. These White Eyes hold no truth within them, and besides, they are stupid. They said they would persuade our brothers, the Utes, to help us and them in the coming battle.''

At this, every Arapaho in the tepee began to laugh uproariously, and Fargo knew why. Hell would freeze over before the Arapahos and Utes ever considered themselves anything other than mortal enemies. Arapahos would rather ride up into the mountains and hunt Utes than go out on the plains and hunt buffalo, even when they were hungry. The Utes were just as foolish on their end.

"Ute brothers?" Niwot continued, directing his speech straight at Fargo and MacFadden. "The only reason the Utes try to steal our women is because their own are so ugly. Instead of hunting like men, Utes grub in the dirt for roots.''

Fargo didn't see how a man who'd just served puppy stew to company had any cause to make fun of Ute diet, but he withheld comment as Niwot concluded. "I spit on them.''

Before they could leave, there were a few more formalities. Some Arapaho warriors took it unfriendly if a male guest refused to spend the night with one of their women. But there was just enough daylight remaining for them to get back to Denver City, so Fargo and MacFadden took a rain check on those generous offers.

Their afternoon ride through the short-grass prairie, back to the twin settlements along Cherry Creek, was uneventful, except for a steady awful wind that roared down from the mountains to the west.

Fargo almost welcomed this latest round of miserable spring weather. Tom was usually as garrulous as an auctioneer on sale day, but this wind was enough to overpower his talkative streak. Freed of any responsibility for making conversation, Fargo studied on what Niwot had said as the Ovaro settled into an easy cross-country walk.

Stephen Dexeter had indeed hauled out his sketching gear at Niwot's Arapaho camp. But if Niwot had been telling the truth—which was likely, Fargo mused, not because Indian tongues were any less forked than white men's, but because the tall chief didn't have anything to gain by lying—then Dexeter's companions had more on their minds than watching him draw pictures.

They were set to rile up the Indians all around these gold camps, Indians who had so far been reasonably peaceful, all things considered. Once those Indians got on the warpath, though, there wouldn't be much choice but to bring out brigades of soldiers from the East.

With the U.S. Army busy fighting Indians, there wouldn't be many soldiers left back East—not enough to put down the rebellion if the southern states decided to leave the union, and there had been a lot of talk about that lately.

That seemed to be Arbuthnot's plan, Fargo decided, but he doubted it had much chance of success. Arbuthnot and his crew were so ignorant about Indians that they just might convince the redskins to join the Blue Sleeves in any future conflicts with the South.

But the white settlers hereabouts were already so stirred up about Indians that just the rumor of a potential Indian uprising could mean disaster all the way around. The Arapaho had pretty much told Arbuthnot to go to hell, but what if those brawlers in Denver City heard that the Arapaho were being encouraged to go on the warpath?

Then some white hothead would surely get up an expedition to go punish the Arapaho for crimes yet to be committed. The Arapaho and their allies, the Cheyenne, would retaliate, inspiring the whites to revenge, and so it would go until a bloody pall covered the high plains from the Yellowstone to the Pecos.

Battalions of federal troops would have to march west then, Fargo thought glumly, and Arbuthnot's murderous plan would succeed, whether or not any Indians went along with it. Fargo felt a little better after he glanced over at MacFadden, who still managed to smile even as the wind was chapping his beardless face.

Content to let MacFadden lead the way, Fargo studied on his next step. The men with Stephen Dexeter were definitely trying to ignite an Indian war, a war that might be started by either side as a result of the Southerners' work. They had to be stopped. Besides that, they'd twice tried to kill him, and Fargo took that sort of thing personally. He'd go after them, which meant he'd be finding Dexeter in the process. He might as well get paid for his trouble, so he reckoned he could take Amelia Parmeter's offer of a job.

Or could he? Who all was in this? There had been Caldwell, now in Boot Hill. Fast-talking Julius Arbuthnot and fancy-dressing Ezekiel Smith were likely headed into the mountains with Dexeter, who might or might not be involved.

Amelia probably wasn't in on it, since they all seemed so dead-set against Fargo's staying alive long enough to get hired. But then again, Fargo didn't trust her. She was so much the southern lady that it was entirely possible she would welcome a chance to further the cause of the glorious South.

As for Stephen Dexeter, who could tell? He was with Arbuthnot and Smith, but was he part of the plan, or just a painter?

It was all a puzzle, but one thing seemed sure to Fargo: He would have to keep an eye on Amelia, and the only way to do that was to take her with him when he went after Dexeter. But just Amelia—not her slaves, nor her brother. He could watch her and still find Stephen, but he didn't want the job of minding four potential enemies while he was tracking down at least a pair, and likely more, of very certain enemies.

Such buildings as the settlements along Cherry Creek offered didn't stop the wind, but they slowed it down to a tolerable roar as Fargo and MacFadden rode up to the livery stable. There was an errand Fargo needed the good-natured MacFadden to run later that night—checking up again on Jeffrey Parmeter. MacFadden said somebody would have to stick around the stable if he was to be out for very long, and Fargo volunteered.

The hayloft sounded positively comfortable, compared to the cabin now that the Parmeter clan had taken it over. Fargo climbed the rickety ladder, spread out his bedroll, and caught up on his sleep.

Fully rested for the first time in a fortnight, Fargo rose with the sun and checked the stalls downstairs. The Ovaro looked fine, and further down the row, he saw that MacFadden's late-night errand had succeeded. Confidently,

Fargo walked the quarter-mile to what was supposed to be his cabin.

The morning air was bracing, but dead-calm. Yesterday's wind had vanished, although it left one good deed in its wake. The gale had sucked the moisture out of the top layer of mud, making walking a good deal more pleasant than it had been on Fargo's last outing on those streets.

He beat on the cabin door until Aphrodite finally peeked out. While Fargo explained that he had to see Miss Amelia immediately, if not sooner, the maid kept trying to switch the subject, asking if he'd seen anything of Mr. Jeffrey, who hadn't come home last night.

Fargo said he wasn't Mr. Jeffrey's keeper, and there was going to be a lot of trouble if he didn't get to talk to Miss Amelia soon. Aphrodite courageously protested that Miss Amelia could not possibly be roused at this ungodly hour, but he persisted until the maid, backing down as always, finally agreed.

Inside the cabin, Fargo found Amelia sitting at the table. In her constant redecorating of the place, she had this time surrounded her bed with suspended blankets. The new arrangement left very little room for Amelia, Fargo, Aphrodite, and Plato, the table, two trunks, the wood stove, the empty galvanized bathtub, and the stacked pile of odds and ends decorating one corner.

"I need to talk to you alone," Fargo muttered, not because what he had to say was particularly private, but because the hovering Aphrodite and hulking Plato made him edgy. Fargo would never understand how people ignored servants and went about their business as if nobody else was there.

Amelia nodded glumly. Hesitating only a moment, she went over and parted the curtain to the makeshift bedroom.

"Interesting setup," Fargo commented, taking a seat on the bed.

Amelia remained standing, her expression making it clear that she wouldn't consider sitting anywhere near him on a bed. "I thought it best if I created separate sleeping quarters before your return," she murmured, turning so he couldn't see her face. "But then you didn't come back last night," she mumbled. "And then Jeffrey left and he didn't come home either. And Plato swears that Jeffrey isn't at that place you call the Columbine. And I've been waiting, and . . ." Amelia faced him again, looking poignantly miserable. "Mr. Fargo, where is my brother?" she wailed.

"We'll find him as soon as you're ready to go," Fargo answered.

"Go?" Amelia whispered.

"I'm hiring on to look for Stephen," Fargo told her. "And you can even come with me."

Amelia's abrupt delight was apparent until Fargo added that her servants couldn't come. "We'll need to travel light and fast," he explained.

"But, Mr. Fargo, you and I cannot travel together unless they come."

"Why not, honey? After the other night, I thought you and I did pretty well together."

"Oh," she moaned. "How could you remind me of that terrible incident? We'll have to take Aphrodite and Plato. And Jeffrey, of course. We'll have to take Jeffrey," she added, already parting the curtains without waiting for Fargo's agreement.

Jumping off the bed, Fargo grabbed her elbow and pulled her back before she managed to pack up herself, Jeffrey, and the two servants. "I'm not taking four tenderfeet," he insisted. "I'd rather go alone."

"I suppose we could leave the servants behind," she admitted. "But not Jeffrey. We must take Jeffrey. But really, Mr. Fargo, must we be in such a horrid hurry that we cannot travel properly?" she asked, her voice just above a whisper.

He had a feeling she didn't trust herself to only one chaperon, after what had happened.

"I suppose not," he conceded. "Have it your way. But if we go slow and Stephen goes steady, this little jaunt might end up a grand tour of the Utah Territory, the Arizona Territory, and points west." Fargo smiled graciously and continued. "Then again, you've never been out West before, and you'll get to meet some grand people. Utes, Jicarilla Apache, Kiowa, Kiowa Apache, Apache, Diggers, Paiutes. Not all of them will be glad to see us, of course," he acknowledged, letting his smile fade, "but nonetheless, they'll be colorful."

It took her but a moment to comprehend the Trailsman's words. Amelia trembled and fell, conveniently landing atop the lace counterpane that covered the bed. Fargo toyed with the notion of relieving her swoon by undoing the whalebone corset, but from the shallow irregularity of her breathing, he knew she'd come around soon.

Her swoon was a sham, something she did to demonstrate that she had been reared in a quality home where young ladies were expected to act properly horrified at the thought of being ravaged by heathen savages.

Amelia was doing her best to reestablish herself as a respectable woman, even if Fargo knew as well as she did what an act her prim, southern-lady routine really was. He had to admit, though, that she had been pretty drunk the other evening, and maybe even a little naive. But she certainly was no straitlaced virgin. And he'd already wasted enough time waiting this morning without having to serve as audience for another of her hypocritical shows.

"Damn," he muttered, knowing she could hear him. "Got to rouse her. But I don't know where they packed the smelling salts." He knelt and stuck his arm under the bed. "Guess this here thunder mug will do the job." Before he could slosh the chamber pot, she was sitting up.

Now that she'd leave the servants behind, all Fargo had to do was persuade her to leave Jeffrey behind, too. He mentioned that they might do well to leave that morning without taking the time to look for her hard-to-find younger brother.

"Why, Mr. Fargo," she countered, "I don't believe I've ever heard such a bold and low proposition in all my born days." As if by command, a blush spread from Amelia's ivory neck to redden her china-doll face. "The very idea of my journeying with you into the wilderness with no chaperon is utterly preposterous. I absolutely insist that Jeffrey accompany us." Breathing unsteadily, with her hand pressed to her breast, the flower of southern womanhood looked ready to swoon again.

She collected herself in moments, though. "I must have a chaperon." Turning her back on Fargo as if the matter was settled, Amelia swept out into the cabin's main "room."

Fargo stared after her, not quite believing she had the audacity to deliver such a performance. But if there was anything Amelia Parmeter didn't lack, it was audacity.

Amelia summoned Aphrodite and told her to start packing for a horseback trip, speaking with a resolve that Fargo dared not interrupt, even though Amelia seemed to have a fast tracking trip confused with a leisurely outing to see some horse races over at the neighbor's plantation. Once outside, Amelia gave additional orders to Plato before Fargo had a chance to persuade her to walk with him over to the livery stable, so they could fetch their mounts.

Just inside the door to the stable office, Fargo conceded that Amelia did have her reputation to worry about, and if it was that all-fired important to her, "then we'll take your little brother. But he'd better be ready to travel right away."

Amelia nodded pleasantly at that as they stepped inside the office to be greeted by Tom MacFadden, who appeared from the back and came to the counter.

"Ah, Skye Fargo himself, as well as a lady. How do you do, Miss Parmeter?" MacFadden swept off his hat with a flourish, flashing a smile at Amelia. "And how might I help you folks this morning?"

"We'll need our mounts, along with her brother Jeffrey's. We're going to the mountains for a few days."

MacFadden stepped back from the counter. "Jeffrey? The two of you and your brother are planning on going to the mountains?" he asked, looking at Amelia.

Amelia nodded expectantly, her happiness showing now that she'd gotten her way over Fargo's objection and Jeffrey would be coming with them.

Her face fell just as fast when MacFadden nodded sadly and said, "Step on back and see for yourselves. You can take your chances, being as there's not all that much law in the territory. But if it was up to me, I'd say you'd be facing a murder charge if you tried to get this man to move any time before next week."

Jeffrey Parmeter, his broadcloth trousers and silk shirt torn and slipping off his body, his cheeks showing a matched pair of bruises not quite covered by the caked blood that spread from under his nose, one tooled-leather boot still on a foot but the wrong foot, lay sprawled across the urine-sotted hay in the stall nearest the front office. Occasional grunting snores emerged from his cut and swollen lips as Amelia lifted her skirts and knelt beside him.

"You needn't worry, though, Mr. Fargo," MacFadden bantered, leaning against a stall wall. "What I hear is that yesterday afternoon, he decided to behave himself, so he figured he'd go back to guarding Clara, like you told him to a couple of nights ago. Guarded her real close, too, and no harm come to either of 'em.''

The easygoing hostler shrugged. "But then the two of 'em stopped over to Uncle Dick's place to celebrate being so safe and all. I happened upon him over there last night myself, after you an' me got back from Niwot's, and I needed a little potion for my windburn.''

MacFadden paused to join Fargo in looking down at the Parmeters. Amelia cradled Jeffrey's head, but there was no evidence that Jeffrey was yet aware of anything in the visible world this morning.

"You know," MacFadden continued, "it's a caution what happens to men who are used to fine sippin' whiskey when they get into that rotgut Taos Lightning over at Dick Wooten's. They brew that stuff out of sugar and pepper and soap, more or less, and I've heard that what Uncle Dick sells as liquor is stuff that even the redskins won't touch. And they ain't none too particular.''

Amelia gently jostled her besotted brother, without success, as Fargo leaned against the splintery stall wall and MacFadden's story continued. "When I come across him, he could still stand up, but that didn't help him a bit. He got up on his feet and announced he could whip any six damn Yankees with one hand tied behind his back.'' Before he could finish the story, Amelia shushed them so she could hear Jeffrey's slurred speech.

"Lemme at them Yankee assholes.'' He rolled his head around, almost falling off the pillow of Amelia's arm, but he had gained some degree of consciousness.

"Such language in front of your sister,'' she berated. "Jeffrey, you are to rise and be my chaperon. Mr. Fargo and I must leave immediately to search for Stephen.''

"Chaperon?'' Jeffrey sat up and shook himself like a dog coming out of the water. The effort caused visible spasms of pain to cross his splattered face. "Jesus, I hurt. The hammers of hell been all over my body and now they're working on my head. I ain't goin' nowhere.''

Fargo and MacFadden looked at each other, trying to keep from laughing at the notion that the boy who had been willing to die for Amelia's good name was not unwilling even to stand up on her behalf.

Amelia stood up to face down her degraded brother, her

voice gaining a hard edge. "Jeffrey, remember that I am a lady. And remember that I am your sister, and that it is your bounden duty to chaperon."

"Leave me alone," Jeffrey slurred. "For all I care, he can fuck you until he splits you in two." He slumped back into the dank straw.

Amelia stood resolutely for a moment before turning around, giving Fargo time to adjust his amused smile into an expression more suitable for her mood. By the time the southern belle looked his way, he matched her grimness.

Fargo felt confident that Tom would continue his fine job of keeping Jeffrey out of the way. And Fargo almost managed to maintain his stern visage for the rest of the morning, until he saw the tiny Miss Parmeter, clad in a full-length camel-hair coat and a plumed hat, sitting sidesaddle atop sixteen hands of prime horseflesh, a sleek bay Tennessee walker that dwarfed its diminutive rider.

"You sure you can handle that big brute, honey?"

"Just as sure as I am that I can handle you, if it becomes necessary, Mr. Fargo." Amelia called the big gelding Odin and whispered to him as if he were a lap dog.

The Trailsman found his familiar perch atop the Ovaro and again admired her bay. Not that he'd ever want to trade mounts, but still, he had to admire quality when he saw it. Amelia's crisp tone interrupted his appreciation. "Mr. Fargo, you said time was of the essence. Just how do you propose to find my Stephen and his companions?"

As the horses stepped smartly—each seemed to be competing to put on the best footwork demonstration—up the rutted wagon road that climbed the gentle rise west of the settlement, Fargo explained that her fiancé's party had spoken of going to Idaho Springs, a mining camp jammed in an impossible valley up Clear Creek. "They have a couple days' start on us," he told her, "but they also have a wagon."

"Just what does that mean?" she inquired. Her voice still had an edge and her face betrayed evidence of hard thought. Likely enough, she had by now realized that her brother's getting shit-faced drunk on the night before she would need him wasn't exactly a coincidence.

They topped the rise, and Fargo paused to scan the countryside, still dominated by winter bleakness although a few determined green patches showed on the prairie. He finally answered her question. "Turn around and take a look at Denver City, or Auraria City, or both, or whatever they call it. See the South Platte coming down from the southwest? And Cherry Creek over there? And how all the shacks are along both sides of Cherry Creek just before it joins the Platte?"

Amelia nodded.

"Now, follow the Platte down a ways, and you'll see a fair-sized creek coming in from the west, the side we're on." Her head turned and she nodded. "That's Clear Creek," he continued. "You can see its course all the way up to the mountains."

The meandering waterway, lined with willows and an occasional bare cottonwood, arced around them to the north and west, where the wayward creek, their road, and the front of the Rocky Mountains all came together. After staring westward for a minute or two, Amelia turned to her companion. "Does that creek just spring out of the mountains? I can't see any valley for it to come from."

"It's not much of a valley," the Trailsman conceded as he nudged the Ovaro into resuming their journey. "It's a steepwalled canyon where the sun hardly ever shines. This time of year it rains rocks when it isn't trying to bury you in mud slides. There's likely still some snow along the way, too."

"And they're taking a wagon up that?"

Fargo grinned. "No, I suspicion not. Look over to your left. The wagon road to Idaho Springs skirts the canyon over there. They have to climb up and down the foothills. It's hard on horses. It's just barely possible to haul a wagon through to the gold camps. But barely possible beats not possible at all."

"Oh, so we won't have to go through that awful canyon." Relief was so evident in her voice that Fargo hated to have to spoil it for her.

"No, we're on horseback, so we do go up the canyon. We might be able to make Idaho Springs tonight, if all goes well. That ought to gain us enough to be within a day or so of them, providing they went there, too. They could have swung farther south and headed for the South Park diggings. Or north to the new strikes up Boulder Creek. Or maybe back to Missouri. But we'll start this way."

Amelia stifled an obvious protest, and that afternoon Fargo

began to wish he had listened to her. The canyon walls loomed over them, dark and forbidding as thunderclouds, and almost as noisy. The roar of the cascading creek echoed off the cliffs, where rocks continually split from where they'd been comfortably sitting since the world started, and bounced down the mountainsides. In the narrowest spots, the pebbles were worse than summertime flies, and more than a few of the tumbling rocks were big enough to lame a horse. So far, they'd been lucky, and the trail, although never more than a yard wide, was better than he'd expected.

They rounded one of the innumerable twists in the canyon and found their way blocked by a crude but effective wooden gate. Next to it, almost filling the only level spot they'd seen since entering the canyon, sat a cabin of fresh-cut logs.

When Fargo shouted, ''Hello, the house,'' about six and a half feet of buckskin-clad stench came out the door. The man was so big that he held his double-barreled ten-gauge shotgun in one hand with the ease that normal men held pistols.

''This here's a toll road now,'' he announced, eyeing the two horses, then ogling Amelia. ''We even got us a charter from the Territory of Jefferson.''

Fargo knew the Territory of Jefferson was the figment of a few overblown imaginations, and had no more right to grant toll-road charters than he did, but he leaned back in his saddle and listened impassively as the man computed their toll.

''Lemme see, two riders and their mounts. Them's horses you don't want to abuse by riding off through the timber. Fact is, you'd want nothin' but the best for them purty mounts.'' After circling them, he stood on the far side of Amelia, maybe a yard away from her. The cabin door was just a few steps behind him, and Fargo, over on the other side, had to look across Odin's withers to see the giant's greedy grin. ''Ten dollars seems fair.''

''Now I know what they mean by highway robbery,'' Fargo replied, waiting to reach into his coat until the man's beady eyes, almost hidden behind a shank of greasy blond hair, moved back to Amelia.

''Funny that folks as can afford fancy mounts allus say they can't afford to put 'em on a good, maintained trail,'' the gatekeeper gabbled. ''But I'm an accommodatin' cuss. It's been a mighty long winter up here, all snowed in and iced up, and a fellow gets a bit tired of his fist. So I'm game for a trade if you ain't got the toll, or even if you do.''

One ham-sized hand moved with speed and precision that a cat might envy. The gatekeeper clasped Amelia's shoulder with bruising force and started to pull her down from the sidesaddle as she twisted like a snake on a griddle.

The giant obviously planned to use Amelia as a shield while he stepped backward to the cabin. But her ability to wiggle slowed his scheme. The big man's other huge arm came up, ready to swing the ten-gauge down across Odin's neck to blast Fargo.

The man was huge, agile, and fast, but not fast enough. Before he could get the scattergun down, his head showed. Fargo put a .44-caliber hole between the man's ears, just above his once-broken hawklike nose, and the unfired shotgun fell between the horses.

For as skittish as Odin had appeared at first, the tall bay was a champ. At any rate, he stayed far calmer amid the noise and blood than Amelia. The giant toll collector went down, pulling her down with him. In a way, his plan had succeeded, except that the lonely lecher wasn't alive to enjoy it.

Under his immense torso, Amelia lay spread-eagled. Her attempts to scream were muffled by the rancid-smelling buckskin that weighed against her gasping mouth. Unable to throw off her burden—he had to outweigh her by at least two hundred pounds—she wiggled, twisted, and bounced as best she could. Instead of falling aside, the corpse stayed aboard and moved along with her.

Lest any strangers happen along and get the wrong idea about Amelia's virtue, Fargo dismounted, grabbed a boot of boat-sized proportions, and pulled on the huge carcass. Along with every other eared creature within a day's ride, he knew when Amelia's face was clear of the awful burden. Fargo wasn't certain that he'd ever heard any sustained sound so shrill and loud; Amelia's desperation made a Lakota war whoop sound like a church whisper.

Considering that she had just been the victim of an attempted rape by an oversized, stinking corpse, Amelia recovered her composure quickly enough. Although it was not all that late in the afternoon, the constricted canyon floor had seen the last of the sun for the day, and the lengthening shadows ominously climbed the gray-brown canyon walls. They didn't stay there any longer than it took Fargo to lever the huge body off the wide spot, down into the jagged rocks that lined the creek.

No matter what that toll-road gatekeeper had charged, Fargo surmised, it would have been too much. Anybody could pay five dollars for a toll-road charter and set up a gate, and most folks didn't do much more than that. Collecting the money seemed more important to them than filling in bogs or widening a shelf or even general cleaning. He and Amelia couldn't make much time at all, thanks to the rocks and recent deadfall strewn across the path. The next mile took the better part of an hour before they were rewarded with an open stretch.

The gloomy canyon floor widened into a sunlit tree-lined meadow. In another month, when the weather warmed up and the high snows began to melt and flow down, this valley would be an impassable bog. But today it was pleasant riding until Fargo's blue eyes, straining into the sun, scanned the mountainside a quarter-mile ahead of them. He caught three bare aspen treetops swaying left and right when all the others were swaying up and down, in cadence with the mild afternoon breeze.

Hoping that Amelia's Odin had as much good sense as he had good looks, Fargo abruptly pointed the Ovaro uphill toward the sparse timber and nudged with his knees. In seconds, he had his new Sharps in hand and had dismounted in such cover as the valley's south-facing side offered. Turning, Fargo pulled Amelia off Odin's back. She was still astonished by her mount's sudden lunge and Fargo's abrupt action when he pushed her down just as the first shot echoed, and echoed, and echoed some more.

Judging by the cannonlike sound and that only one shot had been fired, and that the single round came after, not when, they broke for cover, Fargo knew he faced another big Sharps buffalo gun. A Sharps had range to spare, but it took time to swing it around to a target, and it took more time to reload it between shots. Fargo doubled that estimate within the minute as a peal of man-made thunder boomed up from down-canyon. Trapped in a crossfire, he and Amelia hunkered down behind a fallen ponderosa.

Having caught her breath, Amelia turned to him, wide-eyed, her voice a husky whisper. "Is it possible that that uncouth lout whom you dispatched had friends? And those friends are trying to avenge him now?"

"Go to the head of the class," Fargo replied. "Likely there were three of them. The big one at the gate, the others patrolling, just in case. When these two heard all our noise at the tollgate and then saw us riding on up their private path, they figured out real fast what must have happened."

She silently sidled next to him, her arm reaching across his back. "Mr. Fargo, I owe you an apology for my unladylike conduct. Had I not caused such a commotion, they might never have noticed."

"I'm not accepting your apology," he whispered back. "They'd have heard my gunshot. And I don't see that you had any more choice about the noise you made than I had about the ruckus I made. When you've got something as big and ugly as a grizzly coming after you, you do what you have to. You've got nothing to apologize for."

Fargo stuck his head up as far as he dared, and peered over the log. As he feared, the valley was deathly still. Returning to Amelia's side, he grabbed a stick and sent his hat up atop it. Only one of the .50-caliber slugs found its mark, spinning the hat like a top, but the other came close enough to have taken out a shoulder if it had been Fargo, rather than a stick, beneath the hat. "They're good," he commented. "By the time I could get my sights on one of them, their slugs would cut me into doll rags."

"Couldn't we distract them?" Amelia asked as she huddled against Fargo's prone form. "If they started firing in another direction, wouldn't that give you the opportunity you need?"

"Just how might they be distracted?" Fargo held in his temper, although it was hard to do when he was in a tight spot with someone who insisted on stating the obvious.

"Mr. Fargo, I could distract them if I got on Odin and began to ride away."

"Sure, and the U.S. Cavalry will ride in and save us. Just as soon as you start stirring, the lead will start flying."

The crisp tone that she had employed on Jeffrey an aeon earlier that day returned to her voice. "Mr. Fargo, I'll have you know that I'm a fine horsewoman. I may fall prey to men who conspire to enfeeble my chaperon. I have no talent at remaining silent when a brute is attempting to debauch me. And I may lack your skill with firearms. However, I notice that I am already in mortal danger, which will continue should I remain in this spot. Should my end be ordained, let it come quickly. I can ride, and Odin can take me anywhere I choose to go.'' Before Fargo could hold her still, she rolled away and was running back toward the horses.

However much Amelia trifled with the truth at other times, she had told Fargo no lies about Odin. That big Tennessee walker came about as close to his Ovaro as any horse ever had. Still, he marveled when he rolled around to see Amelia, brush popping beneath her and the first pair of bullets flying by her, leap aboard and take off, parallel to the border between trees and meadows. She and Odin jumped a yard-high deadfall barrier without hesitation, and after a couple hundred yards in the timber, they veered downhill, emerging into the open, her bent-over body presenting a tiny target. Even so, both ambushers fired, their shots going high. Apparently, they were reluctant to hit the splendid bay.

Fargo turned his attention from Amelia to the other side of the valley, where two clouds of blue-white powder smoke slowly rose. The upstream one was nearer, but even so, the range was a good four hundred yards. Fargo stretched as best he could to get the tension out of his legs and back, took a calming breath, and made sure the Sharps was ready. From the snapping of twigs and the squish of soggy aspen leaves under hoof, he knew Amelia had charged back into the timber. When she darted out again into the open, Fargo was ready.

The upstream ambusher straightened himself to fire at his fleeing target. He sat slumped back even more quickly, probably surprised as hell about the half-inch holes that Fargo's Sharps had just put in his chest and back. That shot led to an inevitable puff that announced Fargo's location as surely as if he had raised a flag and saluted it.

Fargo got down behind the log just as the answer arrived from Mr. Downstream, the heavy bullet drilling a good six inches into the soft ponderosa. But that, Fargo knew, would buy a little time for Amelia and Odin. Just what they would do with it, he had no idea. Mr. Downstream, if he had any sense at all, wouldn't be sticking his head out for a while. On the other hand, the ambusher could hardly afford to let Amelia ride away. Enjoying the notion that he wasn't the only one in a predicament, Fargo positioned himself for maximum view with minimum exposure.

Amelia, damn her, was scatting straight across the meadow, headed straight for Mr. Downstream. Odin cleared the rock-lined creek with a spring from his powerful haunches and continued across without breaking stride, even as the hillside steepened and the timber loomed. When she cut to her left just under the trees, Odin turning on a dime and leaving nine cents' change, Fargo saw what he'd been hoping to see.

The ambusher, sure that he had to stop Amelia before the rider came close enough to gun him from horseback, stood up. It was six hundred yards if it was a foot, and even with a well-smithed Sharps and years of experience, shooting got chancy at such distances. That old boy had been damned good, Fargo conceded, to hit the log in front of him. And the hat shot had been even better. All Fargo could do was take his best shot when the ambusher stood and tried to get his sights on Amelia. He fired.

In the smoke, Fargo couldn't see whether he'd hit the ambusher. And it took him a moment to find Amelia, weaving in and out of the tree line, her now-loose hair flying behind her. For all that Fargo could tell, she was enjoying the time of her life out there, and the big bay also appeared to view this outing more as pleasure than work.

For five long minutes, nothing emerged from Mr. Downstream. Fargo whistled for the Ovaro and got astride, but kept himself low as they hastened across the meadow. The pinto jumped the creek easily enough, but not, Fargo suspected, with the grace that Odin had shown.

After spotting where Amelia had last turned into the trees, Fargo felt surprised when she wasn't waiting for him at the first decent cover. Even though her route on into the trees was easy enough to follow, going wherever she'd gone was no picnic. The slope quickly got steeper and more slippery with the normal spring dampness. On this north-facing side of the valley, the vegetation was so thick that Fargo dismounted and padded upward, working to his right.

After climbing for ten minutes, he stopped to perch at a comfortable spot about a hundred feet uphill from a tiny clearing. Fargo enjoyed what he saw. The Trailsman's long shot must have grazed the upstream bushwhacker, a compact fiery-haired man, who stood in the clearing sporting an incongruous salt-and-pepper steerhorn mustache. He also sported a mean red streak across the top of his right arm, which he was groggily clutching with his left hand. Such attention as the carrot-haired marksman had left was devoted to Amelia, who stood a dozen feet away, aiming a shiny nickel-plated derringer at his heart.

"That man you say you're waitin' for is just like every other man, darlin'." Mr. Downstream coughed and got a better grip on his arm. "He's done rode on and left you, if'n he ain't dead by now from that clear shot I got. I tell you, darlin', I don't miss. What happened is he got off a lucky one that stunned me afore he finished cashing in from my shot. I knows it hulled him good. Now, we gonna be friends and help each other out, or what?"

Amelia's measured voice came through clearly. "I hold every confidence that the gentleman will arrive presently. And if he should not join me before sunset, I shall feel no remorse when I do what I must."

"Lady, I ain't done nothin' to you." The man was so busy trying to persuade Amelia that Fargo had no trouble working his way down without their noticing him. "How was I to know that Little Mike brought his troubles on himself back up at the tollhouse? Honest, lady, it's just my job to watch for gate-jumpers and other riffraff trespassers. For all I knowed when Scotty and me heard that ruckus and then seen you two comin' up the creek, your travelin' man had just shot down Little Mike out of pure cheapskate meanness, an' you was a refined lady who got upset and made a fuss about seeing somebody shot right afore her eyes. The first time I seed somethin' like that, I damn near had me a fit, too."

"Not bad, not bad at all," Fargo said as he stepped into the clearing, his own pistol at ready. "But I think you gave a better speech up in Culver City one winter night when they were fixing to hang you."

"Hang me?" The man slowly turned toward Fargo, who was sure, now that he saw the white scar line extending backward from Long-Loop Lem's right eye.

"That was the plan, when they found you with somebody else's horse and without a good excuse. I sure enjoyed it when they let the condemned man have a few last words and you smooth-talked that crowd out of stringing you up."

Fargo leaned back against a convenient boulder and continued. "In those days, you were Luther Jackson, and most folks that read the posters in the post office would probably know you as Lou Pearson, but I recall you best as Long-Loop Lem, the ace buffalo-hunter who never paid for a mount. You're a mean man with that Sharps, Lem, and that had a way of discouraging folks who might want their horses back."

"Skye Fargo. Shit. 'Scuse me, ma'am. I mighta knowed it was you. There's only one man anywheres as could wing me with his buffler gun at that godawful range. An' I had you right in my sights once today, too. How'd I do?"

"Good, Lem, mighty good, considering. About two feet low and maybe half a second late."

"And on that account, I ended up stunned a bit, an' when I come around, here's this filly standin' me down with that whore's gun." At Amelia's harrumph, he stepped back and apologized. " 'Scuse me, ma'am. Nothin' personal. That's just what we calls them little bulldog hideout guns. Now, Fargo, what's gonna happen here? You gonna stand there an' watch whilst she guns me down in cold blood? You gonna do it yourself? Or mebbe you'll do the right thing? You know I was just doin' my job, don't you?"

"Miss Parmeter, what would you consider just in this case?" Fargo inquired, amusement flashing in his lake-blue eyes.

Amelia did not turn her steely gaze from Long-Loop Lem as she answered, "He planned to gun us down in cold blood."

"And he would have gotten one of us, too," Fargo agreed, "if I hadn't grazed him."

From Amelia's effort to maintain a stern countenance, Fargo could tell that his message about her dumb riding stunt was getting through. He went on. "So I say we do the cold-blooded thing. We'll take Lem and Scotty's horses on with us to Idaho Springs, where they were doubtlessly stolen anyway."

"That accounts for the horses, but what shall we do with Mr. Lem?" The man's desperate eyes turned to Amelia as her words came out slowly and clearly. Then Lem looked toward Fargo, who gazed admiringly at Amelia before answering. She was no woman to get crosswise of, he was now certain.

"The cold-blooded thing, of course," Fargo answered. "Peel off your clothes, Lem, starting with the boots. Likely it won't get much below twenty degrees out here tonight. If you keep moving, you should manage to get to your cabin before any important parts of you freeze and fall off."

"You son of a bitch." Lem had enough anger rising in him now to keep him warm all night. "Like hell I'll freeze my pecker off."

"Don't waste our time." Amelia punctuated her icy tone with a wide shot from the derringer. Lem wasn't in any shape to tell just how wide it was, though, and he started tugging at his boots, then his toeless socks, all the while explaining that he'd been raised by upright folks who'd taught him not to take his clothes off around a lady he wasn't married to.

But Amelia wasn't looking. As soon as she had realized that Fargo had the situation under control, Amelia had spun around on her heels, swirling her awesome petticoats. Lifting her chin, she straightened and turned her stiff, haughty back to the sight of the redheaded Lem's pale flesh.

Fargo laughed at the last sight of Lem's bare ass bobbing through the trees in the waning daylight, but not as much as he laughed when Amelia finally got around to asking if it was yet a proper time for her to turn around. "Why, sure," he told her. "We'll have a nearly full moon tonight and I'd like to push on."

She turned to face him as he continued. "Or I suppose we could make camp. Whichever you want. Then you can do what you've a mind to when it's time for me to shuck my duds. But I sure as hell won't be looking the other way when it's your turn."

# 5

Rather than spend the night in the place Long-Loop Lem had threatened to make their last, Amelia elected to go on.

The toll road soon dwindled to more of a nonentity than a fraud. A narrow trail had been cut into the canyon wall, but the precipitous slope above the trail offered an unnerving trickle of slipping wet earth and the constant danger of rock slides. Another trail, meandering along the creek bank, was boggy and choked by willows.

Fargo was surprised by how uncomplaining Amelia was when repeatedly they had to dismount and lead the horses, including those they had taken from Long-Loop Lem, across fields of crusted snow. But maybe that was because she was light enough to stay on top, whereas Fargo nearly always broke through the crust and found himself wallowing.

Worse, the horses didn't like it at all. Although Amelia did her best, only the full power of Fargo's weight, added to his baritone cursing, could move the horses through the drifts. As they moved on, they left behind the steepest part of the canyon where the snow had lingered on the trail in narrow spots that the sun seldom reached.

But the evening soon plunged into one of those lung-freezing, teeth-shattering, jaw-jolting nights only the mountains could provide. The sun set early in the canyon. The moon offered light enough but no warmth. It was cold enough to set Fargo's teeth to chattering, and he was used to the Rockies. He wasn't at all sure a hothouse flower from the South could even survive such brutal cold.

Fargo kept glancing back to make sure Amelia was still following, but when he found she was, he merely pushed on harder, deciding it would be better to get her in out of the cold than to stop and let her rest. Besides, he thought irritably, she would probably only bitch about everything—as if he had controlled the weather, the rock slides, the snowdrifts, and the willows.

Once clear of the canyon, the road joined another; the surface was dry and level and Fargo stepped up the pace. But Amelia fell back.

Glancing around again, Fargo reined in the Ovaro, peering back over Lem's horses to see that he had lost Amelia more than a quarter-mile back. Cursing, he scanned the moonlit vista to see she was ambling, but at least she was still on her horse. Fargo headed toward her.

"You all right?" he shouted, drawing up beside her.

Amelia turned her face toward Fargo, and he could see her features clearly in spite of the half-light. "Oh, yes, I'm fine," she answered, looking a little bit surprised to find him there.

"Something wrong?" he persisted, noting her confusion.

"Oh, no," she denied. "Did I drop behind?"

"You don't know?"

"I'm terribly sorry. It won't happen again." She barely whispered, and yet he could hear her well. To Fargo's amazement, Amelia smiled. "It's just so beautiful, isn't it?" she bubbled.

It was that—with the jagged mountain peaks dark against the gray sky, and wisps of clouds drifting in front of the moon, with stark silhouettes of evergreens looming out of the shadows, and white patches of snow gleaming in the moonlight—but he hadn't expected her to notice. Fargo had more or less figured that his magnolia blossom would have withered from frost nip by now. And he had even been feeling a little guilty about it.

"This isn't a sightseeing trip," Fargo mumbled. He couldn't help but feel annoyed with her. For the past hour, he'd been thinking it might be best to leave Amelia in Idaho Springs. Without her brother and servants she could cause little harm. The more he reflected on the idea, the better he liked it, but then he'd been sure that Amelia would jump at the chance of staying behind after experiencing this bone-chilling ride. Now, he wasn't so sure.

"In case you haven't noticed, it's cold out here," he muttered as he spurred the Ovaro around to head up the road.

Fargo didn't expect any trouble catching up with Arbuthnot, Smith, and Dexeter, but a little time for musing had led him to believe it might be more fitting to trail them for a while. That way, he could check at the post offices along the route and see if they were sending messages home. He could watch and see if the Southerners were joined by others.

Maybe he could even find out how involved Dexeter was. Stopping Smith and Arbuthnot wouldn't do much good if there were legions of Southerners sharing their mission. But trailing the southern conspirators would mean he was facing a much longer, more vigorous trek than the one he had invited Amelia to come along on.

Fargo wasn't sorry he had brought her. Left in Denver, Amelia would almost certainly have launched an expedition to follow him. She would probably try to do the same thing if he left her in Idaho Springs. But perhaps the motley assortment of prospectors and hard cases available for hire there would daunt her. After all, in Idaho Springs she would be all alone, without the hulking black man or her brother to interrupt any hanky-panky.

On the other hand, if he left Amelia behind, she would most likely find some way to follow him, unless he convinced her otherwise. As he rode, Fargo imagined attempting to talk Amelia into letting him ride out without her, and it was then that he began to realize he could trust the woman . . . to plague him.

The road curved, and the lights of Idaho Springs came into view. Terraced into the mountainside, the town seemed to be stacked like bricks, one building atop another. Still a half-mile from the hamlet, Fargo veered off toward the closest lighted structure, the Freighters' Inn. It looked much like any other stage station—a two-story, wood-frame building with a sharply sloping roof—except there was no regular stage to Idaho Springs as yet.

Inside, the place was pretty near hot, and it was pungent with the smell of just-baked bread. Three long tables covered in white linen filled the dining area, and a huge fireplace dominated the far side of the room. Although it was getting late for dinner, about thirty men crowded around the first two tables, which Fargo figured meant the food was either real good or real cheap, and he hadn't ever come across anything underpriced in a mining camp.

Aside from the men at the tables, another dozen or so lolled around the fireplace absorbing the heat. He and Amelia stood in the entrance, still unnoticed by the crowd of diners. Behind her back, a board cluttered with dozens of tacked-up announcements touted the arrivals and departures of freighters' wagons, pack teams, mule trains, ox carts, and the like. Idaho Springs was obviously booming, but it was still early in the season. In another month or so, the mountains would be as overrun as Denver, and day and night places like the inn would be full of men crammed together like crated cargo. But in the meanwhile, he just might be able to find her a decent place to stay.

Fargo glanced over at Amelia. Her cheeks were chapped a flaming red. Stepping in front of her, he pulled off his glove and cupped her face in his hand to rub his thumb across the damaged skin. "It's not so bad," he told her, finding that her flesh was reddened but not rough.

"No, of course not," she sighed, abruptly sagging up against Fargo as she stared at him with eyes that made a lie of her primness.

Startled, Fargo pulled away, dropping an arm around her shoulder to lead her into the dining room. "There'll be time for that, later," he muttered gruffly, wondering if she could read his mind. Did Amelia know he was planning on leaving her behind?

"Unhand me, sir," she rasped, suddenly bristling. "I wouldn't want to give you or these gentlemen the wrong impression."

Immediately realizing Amelia knew nothing of his thoughts and had merely given in to her warmer nature for a moment, Fargo would have laughed—if every man in the room hadn't turned their way. The men ogling them couldn't have looked more stunned if Fargo had been accompanied by a band of Comanche. In Denver, the ratio of men to women was about ten to one, while most mining camps were lucky to boast a woman for every fifty men. And Amelia was the kind of woman who got gawked at when the odds were even.

Seeing so many men, all of them goggling at her as if she were more important than the queen of England, Amelia instinctively summoned one of her brightest smiles.

"Don't encourage them," Fargo warned lowly.

"Encourage them?" she huffed. "I'm merely being courteous."

"Courteous?" Fargo scoffed. "If you ask me it's more like carnivorous."

Chafing, Amelia stalked toward the fireplace, and the crowd gathered there parted as miraculously as the Red Sea. With a scathing backward glance at Fargo, Amelia turned her attention to her new admirers. "Why, thank you, gentlemen," she fluttered as they made room for her near the hearth. She turned her smile on one man, then another, then another, and another. Her words brought the men out of their trance.

"Could I get you something hot to drink, ma'am?" one man offered.

"Could I take your coat?" another piped.

"Abby, where's Abby?" an old reprobate shouted. "There's a lady here needs tending to."

The men clamored, all talking at once, while a boy scrambled to get a chair, elbowing his way through to set it in front of the fire for Amelia. Smiling radiantly, she held out her hand to him so he could help her be seated.

But faced by the kind of woman he'd never seen before, the boy mistook the gesture and grabbed up Amelia's hand, kissing it passionately. He'd no sooner let go than another took her hand, a bald, grizzled, swaying drunk who slobbered several more kisses before he lost his place. Amelia whirled toward Fargo, her face showing her growing alarm, just as the horde closed in around her like swarming bees anxious to get a taste of nectar. Laughing, Fargo decided it wouldn't hurt her any to get a little drool on her fingers. And maybe next time she would be a bit more careful with her smiles.

Although he wasn't too happy to see so many men crowding in and jabbing at one another, Fargo doubted they meant Amelia any harm.

Normally there were only two kinds of women in mining camps, sporting women and the few somewhat worn, usually overtired wives who had ventured out with their husbands. Although they were ridiculously outnumbered, the wives were the ones who almost always ended up doing all the laundering, sewing, cooking, and cleaning a couple of hundred men needed. So even though there probably wasn't a seedier, more unlikely-looking bunch of hand-kissers on the continent, Fargo knew that if the men were overeager, it was only because it might be months before they came across another pretty, well-dressed woman who was willing to smile at them without charging.

Relieved to know there was at least one other woman around, Fargo went in search of Abby, but as it turned out, Abby, the proprietor's daughter, wasn't a day over twelve. She came bustling out of the kitchen carrying a basket of bread and muffins, then went rushing back in to lug out a heavily laden tray. Fargo helped her with the tray and took the opportunity to ask about accommodations in town.

Abby was not only young, she was inordinately shy. Much more cautious than Amelia, she stood far back from Fargo, answering his questions with her gaze glued to an imaginary spot on the floor.

"You seen any Southerners?" he asked. "An older gentleman, a bit paunchy, but dressed pretty fancy. And two others. A yellow-haired man and a dark-haired man with a mustache. Kind of dandified?"

"I heard tell of some like 'em in town," she mumbled. "Ain't seen 'em."

"Here," Fargo said, tossing her a coin. For the first time, Abby looked up. A pretty little redheaded girl with lots of freckles, she grinned as she caught the dollar.

"Could you get me and the lady some hot coffee before you bring the food?"

"That lady's with you?" the little girl blurted, glancing sideways to look at the crowd gathered at the fireplace.

"Well, she was," Fargo admitted, laughing.

Abby turned and studied Fargo with wistful, serious intensity. "And she's over there with them, when she's got you? She's a fool, mister," Abby proclaimed solemnly. "When I grow up, I'll know better."

Before Fargo could think of a suitably modest reply, Abby spun around and rushed back into the kitchen.

"Amelia," Fargo boomed as he took a seat at the empty table. He could tell Amelia stood up because the men fanned back slightly, but the multitude wasn't as willing to part to let her out as they had been to let her in.

Finally, Amelia staggered out of the crowd, a man on each arm, both of them holding her elbows so high they nearly lifted her off the floor. But Fargo had to admit she was holding up pretty well, still smiling and nodding. "Why, thank you, sir," she whispered. "Why, that was most gracious."

Somehow, Amelia managed to keep smiling and nodding and uttering idiotic pleasantries until she broke away. But her dress had obviously been well-trampled as she sat on her throne. Dusty footprints and mud decorated the hem, and Fargo noticed that Amelia was unconsciously rubbing her overkissed hand in the folds of her skirt. By the time Amelia sat down, both her coffee and her food were getting cold.

Knowing full well that most of her ingratiating charm toward the men was calculated to annoy him, Fargo ignored Amelia as he finished his meal. It was pretty hard not to laugh out loud, smirk, or say "I told you so" whenever a man came up with some new pretense to bother her, but Fargo acted like he didn't even notice the disruptions.

The miners were incorrigible, but they weren't stupid. They knew damned well that they were driving Amelia crazy, but as long as she was going to keep smiling, they were going to keep her from eating. Three more characters stepped up to tell Amelia that they'd never had a more enjoyable evening, and Fargo realized they wouldn't have been any more interested in Amelia if she were stark-naked.

"Would you kindly pass the butter?" she asked icily.

"Sure," Fargo agreed, barely bothering to glance at her before he pushed it across the table.

"Are we taking rooms here?" Amelia inquired.

"Here?" Fargo muttered, looking up from his food to scan the dining room. "I doubt they've got more than one room. And a common room, of course." Suddenly, he grinned. "But then, maybe you wouldn't mind sharing a room with ten or twelve of these fellows. They sure wouldn't mind sharing one with you."

"How dare you?" Amelia gasped. Angrily, she turned on Abby, who approached to freshen Fargo's coffee. "Do you have a private room available?" Amelia demanded.

The girl shrank back at Amelia's grim tone. "Yes, ma'am," she mumbled.

"Only one?"

"There's only one here," the girl blurted, obviously disconcerted by Amelia's angry glare.

"I'll take it," Amelia stated.

"Yes, ma'am," Abby agreed. "I'll show you and your husband upstairs right after you eat."

"My husband?" Amelia snapped. "This man is certainly no husband of mine."

"Why, honey," Fargo interjected, reaching out to pat Amelia's hand consolingly, "surely you aren't planning on turning me out in the cold."

Abby started to interrupt, but Fargo waved her to silence. "Don't worry about my friend," he told the little girl. "She's a mite touchy. So why don't you just get the room ready?" Abby hurried away, happy to escape, and Fargo turned back to Amelia.

"Why, you . . ." Amelia choked. "As far as I'm concerned, sir, you can sleep out in the stables, where you belong."

"But I'd rather sleep with you."

"Would you keep your voice down, sir?" Amelia hissed.

Fargo shrugged. "Well, I guess I'll just have to leave you alone tonight," he announced resolutely, trying to look properly chagrined by Amelia's rejection although he felt like hooting in triumph as he pushed his chair back. "I'll see you in the morning," he called as he went out the door, leaving a sputtering Amelia behind.

Fargo mounted the Ovaro and rode directly to the hotel that Abby had assured him offered the best accommodations around. The recent storms had delayed the spring rush into the mountains. The wagon road into Idaho Springs had been left not only muddy, but washed out in some places and covered by rock slides in others. Although the route was rumored to be passable, it would be tortuous for anyone wanting to haul in supplies. With some smugness, Fargo reflected on how lucky that was for him. First, because Arbuthnot, Smith, and Dexeter had probably been among the tortured when they hauled in their load of sugar and tobacco. Second, because there'd be rooms at the hotel.

Twenty minutes later, after he had already checked in, Fargo stood in the hotel lobby surveying the place. It wasn't much, but it was better than the only hotel with vacancies in Denver. That place hadn't been much more than a barn that profited by jamming six or eight strangers into every stall. Sauntering over to the desk, Fargo studied the clerk, a man in his early twenties clad in Levi's and flannel. Lacking the obsequious politeness of a proprietor, the young clerk was in all probability merely biding his time while he scraped up another grubstake.

"I was supposed to meet some friends here, but I'm a few days late. Three southern gentlemen, one elderly, one fair, one dark. All a bit foppish?" Fargo ventured, thinking the Southerners had probably stayed in the town's best hotel.

"They was here, but they left."

"Did they say where they were going? Or leave any messages?" Fargo asked, hoping he just might get lucky and intercept a message meant for someone else.

"Nope," the clerk denied, but then he smiled. "But they sat in the lobby one night talking about Middle Park."

"Where's that?"

"Over them mountains," the clerk answered, waving his hand in a general northwest direction.

"It's not very far?"

"Maybe thirty or forty miles if you was a hawk. A couple hundred if you can't fly."

"Aw, shit," Fargo groaned, but then he shrugged. "Are there big strikes over there?" he inquired.

"None at all that I know of. They was talking about painting Injuns." Rolling his eyes, the desk clerk laughed. "Seems to me the Injuns do a pretty good job of painting themselves," he said, but immediately his amusement faded as he told Fargo, "Your friends better hope them Injuns ain't wearing war paint."

Fargo thought it might make things simpler if "them Injuns" were wearing war paint, but he couldn't rely on it. After discussing the around-hell-and-back routes into Middle Park, which seemed to be the only ways to get there, Fargo went to the closest saloon. The bar ran all the way down the left side of the room, taking advantage of an old superstition that drunks invariably staggered to the left.

The only tables there were gaming tables, so to be comfortable a man either had to lean on the bar, where he would inevitably drink more, or he could lounge at the tables. With the wagon road being so difficult, the only liquor available had been doctored. Fargo could taste the taint of sugar, pepper, and raw alcohol on his tongue. The local version of Black Bug Blood was potent enough and it really wasn't too unpleasant, although Fargo was fairly sure anyone who drank much of it would be dead by morning.

There were a few chairs scattered about, and Fargo pulled one up against a support post nearly center to the room. With a drink in hand, he sat back, listening. The men hereabouts seemed to have reduced the wilderness into the dimensions of a small town. Before too long, Fargo knew who was prospecting up which gulch, who was panning down which creek, and who was traveling on which trail.

Rising, he stretched and ambled over to the bar. "Hey, mister," he addressed a bandy-legged, bewhiskered old sot. "I couldn't help overhearing you tell of some pompous, wise-ass southern gents. I was supposed to deliver some supplies to some that sure would fit that description. But they don't seem to have waited around for me. Could you tell me where you ran into them?"

The old man not only told Fargo exactly where to find the Southerners, he added a deprecatingly colorful depiction of Julius Arbuthnot.

"You talking about that bushy-eyed fellow?" a lean man of about thirty interjected. "Why, he's the one that shot Tony, here," he accused, slapping his dark-eyed companion on the back as he gestured toward the arm Tony wore in a sling. "Said he wouldn't take insults from no darkie. Tony didn't insult him, did you, Tony?"

"No," Tony explained. "I offer Señor Julius good price on horse, and he say call him Meester Arebutt. I call heem Meester Arebutt, he shoot me."

"Would have killed Tony, too," the companion added, "if that horse hadn't shied and knocked his aim off. Loco and tetchy, that's what that man is. Plumb loco."

Several others had similar accounts of the Southerners' mean disposition toward folks they considered their inferiors, and then the talk turned to mining matters.

Fargo returned to his chair where he closed his eyes, rested his head against the post and tried to sort out his plans. But he'd no sooner begun to muse than he was brought up short by the unmistakable intonation of sermonizing.

Fargo opened his eyes, and sure enough, there was a preacher standing in front of the saloon's nude painting. The man had undoubtedly chosen that place because there was a little raised platform and a roped-off area to keep the customers from leaning on the artwork, but the reverend looked a mite incongruous with his head just about level with the lady's crotch. The painted woman rose above the black-clad, stiff-collared little man. She was an enormous expanse of fleshy white, way too hippy, and decidedly too flat-chested, but still rather sensuous.

"Now, I got nothing against a little diversion," the minister boomed out in a voice much too big for his diminutive stature. "But I want you boys to remember, even our Lord Jesus was tempted in the wilderness."

Fargo glanced around to see what the customers were making out of the minister's appearance, but the men seemed to accept the sermon as just another form of entertainment. They were all paying attention, although they were a bit rowdier than a regular church crowd. A few stamped their feet, several called out, "Amen, brother." One whooped out, "But Hallelujah for the sisters." Looking around, Fargo had the feeling that barroom preaching was an ordinary event in Idaho Springs.

"Now, what we need in this town is a church," the little minister shouted. "A church would bring in good women, and girls like the ones you left back home."

If most of the men hadn't been on their feet at the bar already, they would have given the preacher a standing ovation for that line. The men hooted and hollered, as pleased by the reverend as they might have been with dancing girls.

"I know you're all lonely," the little man roared. "The nights are cold up here. What you all need is a good woman, a woman who will lead you on the path to redemption, not on the road to sin."

"Hey, let us have a little sin," a man shouted.

"Yeah, we like sin," the crowd chorused.

"No, you don't like sin," the preacher bellowed back. "Sin is a woman who will empty a man's pockets for ten minutes of her time. A woman like that is an abomination. The Bible says a woman should cleave on to her man. A church would bring real women, godly women, but a church takes money," the reverend warned.

"Anything for cleaving," a young man shouted, tossing the preacher a coin.

"Yeah, we all want some cleaving," several voices echoed

as the minister moved out into the room, holding his hat high to collect donations.

"Give the preacher some money," a brawny, bearded man demanded as a scrawny fellow moved out of the way.

"Hell, no. I ain't giving him no money," the skinny man refuted. "I got a wife out in Illinois. Just the kind of woman the preacher's wanting to bring in. Far as I'm concerned, she and all them like her can stay in Illinois."

"You going to be stingy after the preacher talked to us so nice like?" the big, brawny fellow questioned.

To Fargo's amazement, the puny man swung, landing a good hard punch right in the big man's belly. The husky giant was nearly doubled over when a third man, seeing no reason to lose the advantage over such a hulking beast, delivered a hammer blow to the big man's head.

"What'd you do that for?" another man shouted, swinging at the third man as the husky guy went down.

Fargo didn't think he had ever seen anyplace as ripe for brawling as these new mining camps. Even the little minister was getting into the fracas. The reverend had cornered a man just about his own size and was prodding him with a forefinger to the chest. The man seemed disinclined to fight, until the preacher landed a fierce uppercut against his jaw. The two of them grappled, then went down, rolling out of Fargo's sight.

Not wanting to get involved in another purposeless brawl, Fargo stood up and was turning toward the door when a man careened his way. Since the brawl was still pretty much confined to the front half of the barroom, Fargo thought he could avoid involvement—if he could just get out without punching, shoving, or decking someone. Moving fast, he swung his chair between himself and the man teetering toward him. Fargo knew if he took the time to wrestle with the man, the fight would surround them, and he wouldn't get out until it was over.

Fargo's chair hit the reeling man square in the back of the knees, and he landed very neatly, almost as if he had intended to sit there. Before the man gained his equilibrium, Fargo was gone.

But back at the hotel things didn't look much better. When Fargo arrived, there were only three men in the lobby besides himself, and two of them were facing off with mutinous expressions that indicated they were about to go for each other's throats.

"I told you," one of them shouted. "I'm taking care of the lady's bags."

"I seen her first," the other one snarled, swinging.

Unfortunately, the lady in question seemed immobilized by the scene. A sweet-looking plump little brunette, she stood like a statue, right behind the taller of the two men, where she was bound to get hurt. And the hotel clerk wasn't being any help at all; he watched as if it were a variety show staged for his benefit.

Fargo rushed over to pull the woman out of the way, but just as he got there, the husky little scrapper threw a second punch and the taller man feinted. There was nothing Fargo could do to protect the little woman but step in the way of it. He felt the fist slam into his shoulder, but he stood as still as the woman, hoping the little guy wouldn't notice him. He had no such luck.

"Why, you son of a bitch," the husky little man screamed. "You sure as hell wasn't here first."

"No," the taller one agreed. "He ain't got no call to be anywheres near her."

Fargo could feel his temper rising when, to his astonishment, the little guy jumped on his back, pounding on his shoulders and kicking at his sides as if he were riding a bronco. Fargo straightened, grabbed the man's hands, and tossed him off with one easy motion, wheeling around almost instantaneously. His icy-blue glare froze his opponents.

"Why, you stupid bastards," Fargo raged, "this here's a woman. She isn't a mining claim. You can't keep her just because you staked out her carrying cases. And you . . ." Fargo spat, shifting his glare to the little man staggering up from the floor. "Do I look like a horse to you?"

The husky man shrank back, but Fargo continued, flexing his hand as he spoke. "Now, if you two still want to fight, that's fine with me," he announced levelly. "But I'd prefer a gunfight."

"I ain't no gunman," the taller one objected.

"That's fine with me, mister." Fargo shrugged. "Truth is, I'd rather see your carcass buried than patched up."

"We ain't fighting," the little one whined.

"Fine," Fargo snorted. "Then get your asses out of here before I kick them off."

The two men looked at each other, but when Fargo took a step forward, they both hightailed it out the door.

"Are you all right, ma'am?" Fargo asked, turning back to the woman.

She wasn't much of a woman at all. At the most she was sixteen or seventeen years old. And she looked more than a little dazed.

"I'm sorry," she whispered, raising her round, glistening brown eyes to look up at Fargo. "It's just that my Billy was killed in a fray like this, not two weeks ago. Busted his head on a stone hearth."

"Ma'am, were you going to check in?" Fargo prodded, glancing at her fought-over luggage.

"Oh, of course," she mumbled.

Fargo picked up her two bags and carried them to the desk. "The lady needs a room," he ordered.

"It'll be fifteen dollars," the desk clerk said.

The girl was real cute, with a little upturned nose and huge brown eyes, but she was pale, and she turned even paler when the clerk revealed the price. "I can't pay that," she said.

"Got a cot in a kind of closet room for twelve," the clerk offered.

The girl only shook her head as she reached over to pick up her cases.

"Oh, hell, I'll pay for it," Fargo muttered.

"I can't let you do that, mister," the girl protested. "Them prices is robbery, nothing less."

Fargo couldn't help but agree, but he couldn't just let the girl walk out into the night, either. Taking her luggage from her, he followed her out onto the hotel's long, covered porch. "You sure you won't let me get you a room?"

"I'm sure," she answered staunchly.

"All right," Fargo agreed. "But look, I've got a room and a bedroll. We could share the room and I'll sleep in the bedroll. I won't bother you any."

The girl studied him for several minutes before she gave a quick nod of assent. "My name's Becky O'Banyon," she said, holding out her hand timidly.

"Skye Fargo," he answered, taking her arm and directing

her toward the fire escape. Unfortunately, she wasn't the kind of girl to face a leering desk clerk.

Fargo couldn't believe he had given up his bed again. Given his druthers, he would rather have paid for an extra room, but he knew she wouldn't let him. With more than a few misgivings gnawing at him as he helped the girl up the rickety outside stairway of the hotel, Fargo started to suspect that a little bit of Jeffrey and Amelia Parmeter was rubbing off on him, and he had no idea whether that would make him more of a gentleman or just more of a hypocrite.

Becky O'Banyon wasn't what Fargo would consider a pleasure to have in the bedroom. She stood with her back to the dresser and her eyes to the door, although she glanced at Fargo every few seconds as if she had to keep track of him. He had the impression she thought he might jump up from behind and bite her.

"I already had dinner, honey," he commented as he settled on the little settee, a flimsy, ornate, sweet-looking piece of furniture that might have looked nice in a parlor house.

"What?" Becky gasped.

"Nothing, honey. What are you doing in Idaho Springs?"

"Going home," she mumbled.

"Where's that?"

"St. Mary's," she answered.

"Your folks live there?"

"Uh huh." She nodded.

"Not much of a talker, are you?"

"No," she agreed.

Fargo stood up. "Maybe I'd better leave for awhile so you can get dressed for bed."

Becky nodded again. Looking up at him, she smiled, but her smile was so fleeting Fargo wasn't sure he believed it had really been there. He gave Becky about twenty minutes before he returned, carrying the bedroll.

She was staring at him, and he hadn't the vaguest idea what he should say to her. He wanted to strip down for bed, but the lantern was on and Becky made him feel more self-conscious than he'd ever been before. Maybe it was because he seldom promised to leave a woman alone; it was a trying experience.

Becky was sitting up in bed, with the covers pulled up around her waist. She had on a flannel nightgown with little pink flowers, and her curly brown hair was loose but pushed back away from her shoulders to tumble down across the pillow. She looked a bit young for his taste, but she was busty enough to prove herself a woman, and a pretty one at that.

Fargo dropped the bedroll and started to spread it out.

"Mr. Fargo, I can't let you sleep on the floor," she whispered.

Fargo looked up and Becky pulled the bedspread back as she moved toward the wall to make room for him.

"I can't sleep there. Not without—" he started to protest, but Becky interrupted him.

"I know," she said.

"You sure?" he asked. Fargo couldn't believe he had asked. He wasn't one to pass up opportunities, but she looked a bit nervous. She was pressing herself back against the wall as if she thought she could push hard enough to get out on the other side.

"I'm sure," she murmured.

Fargo slipped into the bed, but Becky didn't budge away from the wall. And his idea of romance didn't include prying a woman loose from the wallpaper. "You seem kind of scared," he commented.

With her eyes downcast, Becky let out a long, drawn-out, melancholy sigh. "I ain't never done nothing like this," she admitted.

"You've never done it?"

"What?" she asked, glancing up at Fargo.

Fargo rolled his eyes, letting out a sigh for himself as he settled back against the pillow. He certainly didn't want to explain it to her. Considering the kind of women men usually found in gold-rush areas, he sure seemed to be having peculiar luck meeting up with both Amelia and Becky.

"Oh, that," Becky finally realized, smiling. She even started to laugh, but then her color rose up and overheated the reaction. "I didn't mean that. I meant seducing. I never seduced nobody before."

"Is that what you're doing? Seducing me?" Fargo asked, trying hard not to laugh at her. Except for a twitch or two, he pretty much succeeded, but it was the hardest thing he'd ever done.

"Ain't it?" Becky raised her eyes questioningly.

Her eyes were huge, with long, thick lashes. Fargo smiled. "I guess it is," he admitted. As seductions went, he thought her method a mite strange, but it was definitely starting to have an effect.

Becky actually grinned. "I know it ain't right, but I'm glad," she told him decisively.

Remembering what she had said in the lobby about Billy, Fargo realized that was probably what Becky was doing in a mining camp. She had most likely run away with some kid.

Fargo smiled back at her. Becky was a tiny little thing, but plump enough to have well-rounded curves. Her breasts looked downright generous nestled beneath the flannel. It was unfortunate, what had happened to Billy, but Fargo figured that the kid had at least enjoyed a couple of nice things beforehand.

"I wouldn't say it wasn't right," Fargo said, reaching out and pulling Becky toward him. She settled against his chest, wiggling closer as he pulled her down with him. "I'd say it feels just about right. Better than right," he mumbled as he slipped his hand up under her nightgown.

Becky wasn't a very innovative lover. She pulled her nightgown up over her head and tossed it on the floor. But then she flipped over on her back, tugged the covers up over both of them, and squeezed her eyes shut.

But Fargo could tell she liked it. She trembled when he brushed her thighs, shivered when he caressed her breasts, and actually shook when he rubbed her belly.

She was hesitant with her hands, they fluttered lightly on his shoulders, but her hold tightened when he licked her nipples, and her nails dug in when he slipped his hand between her thighs. She even started to moan, but she held back.

For someone who wanted to be a seductress, the girl was sure careful about not acting shameless. She responded easily, though. Her fingers gripped harder, her eyes squeezed tighter, and she let out breathy moans that made her clamp her mouth shut and grit her teeth. She lay on her back without squirming or writhing or rocking. Instead, every time she seemed about to lose control she pressed her soft little ass to the mattress and held her breath.

Becky was ready, and he was long past ready. Fargo rolled on top of her. He heard her breath quicken and saw her grimace as she clenched her teeth, fighting for constraint. And he couldn't do it.

She was too much of a challenge. He was going to get that moan out of her, and he didn't want to be caught up in his own groaning when he did. Fargo wanted to see it happen. Rolling back onto his side, he went back to work. He used his hands, alternately stroking, massaging, and kneading, and followed with his tongue, starting at her earlobes and nibbling, licking and swirling his way down. She was moaning by the time he got to her breasts.

She was moaning, all right, but moaning wasn't enough anymore. Men built dams, harnessed rivers, and stopped up millstreams. But Fargo didn't want to do any of those things, he wanted to free something, just one little thing. It was the opposite of breaking a horse. He wanted to see Becky wild. He didn't exactly want to turn Becky into Clara. But then he didn't really think there was any danger of that.

Fargo had never before felt quite so enthusiastic about foreplay. Becky started squirming and Fargo swirled his tongue around her belly while his hands fondled her sides, her hips, and her thighs. He was into it; it was like betting on a horse race and winning, or getting shot at when the bullet missed, or coming across water in the Nevada desert after you'd just about given up. He moved lower and Becky's moaning turned into screaming. Then, she arched, tensed, and let out a sound that must have woken everybody in the hotel and the adjoining buildings. Laughing, Fargo moved up and slid himself inside of her.

Becky's eyes flew open. "Now?" she whispered.

"Now," he answered.

It was too bad she was a little girl from the Kansas Territory. Becky should have tried ballroom dancing. She followed him real close, anticipating his moves. She was smooth and graceful, but she was good at keeping up the pace. Fargo figured that was a talent she had always had, but he was gratified to hear her rapid breathing escalate into a low rumble that reminded him of purring.

She stayed right with him. He felt the tension building like a storm, and she made a sound that rolled like thunder. Fargo thrust harder and faster, and she clamped her thighs around him. While her whole body—inside and out—trembled like aspen leaves, Becky howled like gusting wind. Fargo struck hard.

Slamming into him with her hips high off the bed, Becky seized up tight, pulling him loose. And she shrieked as if she'd been hit by lighting. Her screeching was high and shrill, carrying up past what humans can hear and lingering. A few people might have even slept through it, but it was definitely uninhibited. Easing off her, Fargo wished there was some way to save sounds and play them back. It would have been nice to hear it all again.

He got up and turned off the lantern before he crawled back into bed. It felt real good when Becky snuggled back against him, but then she made the last noise he wanted to hear.

"Something wrong?" he muttered, knowing she was crying, but not feeling particularly anxious to find out why.

"It ain't fair," she sniffed. "I was only married three months." Becky twisted around in Fargo's arms and pressed her hot little body up against his. "My Billy, he weren't no expert like you, but we was learning. We might have got really good. But now my folks is expecting me to come back home and live like an untouched little girl."

Fargo tried hard to be sympathetic. After all, she was talking about a dead man, and probably a damned young one at that. The realization might have been sobering, if her breasts and belly weren't straining against him.

"Oh, Mr. Fargo," Becky whimpered, "I'm being so terrible. Poor Billy's gone, and I just keep fretting about myself. But sleeping all alone these past eight nights makes me want so bad I ache. Poor Billy," she wailed.

"There's nothing you can do for him," Fargo muttered, soothing her back and shoulders with his palms. "But I'm sure you made him real happy while you could."

"You really think so?" she asked, wriggling closer.

"Uh huh."

"Mr. Fargo, if you was ever to be in St. Mary's . . . ?" Becky left the question hanging.

"I'd come and see you," he finished for her. "But it won't do me any good. By the time I can get done out here and get out there, it'll be too late. The men in St. Mary's aren't going to leave a pretty little thing like you sitting on a shelf." Fargo was telling her the truth. Considering her laments, he doubted she'd stay a widow more than a few weeks. "I reckon you'll be married by summer," he mused.

"You really think so?" she asked, shimmying closer in a way that made her belly jiggle against his groin.

"Yes," he breathed. "But since you seem to consider me an expert, why don't you let me teach you a little more first?"

"Now?" she asked.

"Now." he answered.

In the morning, Fargo put Becky on a mail wagon headed toward Denver. "Are you sure this rig will hold up?" he questioned. "I've heard the road's pretty bad."

"I was up it two days ago," the driver answered. "The road's crumbled away and narrow in places, but this little cart won't give no trouble."

Becky sat up beside the man smiling. She looked a hundred percent happier than she had when Fargo had first seen her in the lobby. "I won't forget you, Mr. Fargo," she called back as the wagon started to move. She twisted around, smiling and waving, with the sun shining in her hair, making him wish he had more time to spend tutoring her. "I'll never forget you, Skye Fargo. Not as long as I live," she shouted back.

It made a man feel good, knowing he'd done something for a woman, something she considered important and lasting.

When Fargo got to the Freighters' Inn, he felt more than ready to back down Amelia. He found her in the dining room in front of her breakfast, not eating it, just stirring it up with her fork.

Fargo sat down on a chair across from her. "Miss Parmeter," he announced, "this trip's going to take a little longer than I thought, so I'm leaving you here."

Amelia looked up at him and all the color drained from her face. "But, Mr. Fargo, I told you how imperative it is that I find Stephen as soon as possible. I explained it to you," she protested.

But having her condition pointed out to him didn't further her cause. Having a woman along was bad enough, a pregnant one was unquestionably bad. "I don't need a woman fainting on the trail," he muttered.

"Why, sir, I've never fainted in my life."

"Really, Miss Parmeter?" he said tightly. "Then what was that little exhibition you staged back at the cabin all about?"

The blood surged back to her cheeks in a flash flood. Amelia looked not only embarrassed; she looked almost contrite. "It won't happen again." she whispered.

"No," he agreed. "Not with me around."

"Oh, please, Mr. Fargo," she begged, her eyes filling with tears. "Please, sir. Don't you understand? I have to go. I have to." Amelia leaned over the table and grabbed his arm to press her lips against his hand. Then she looked up at him with wet, blue, pleading eyes.

Fargo had seen enough tears lately. He had felt good when he came into the inn, and he didn't like having his mood dampened. Besides, he figured by the time they arrived in Breckinridge, Amelia would want to stay behind. "Aw, shit," he mumbled. "Come, if you have to."

Amelia was up and around the table. "Thank you, Mr. Fargo. Thank you," she effused, throwing her arms around his shoulder and kissing him. Her gratitude wasn't quite on a par with Becky's, but it was close. On the other hand, knowing Amelia, it wouldn't last too long.

# 6

Riding into the high mining camp of Breckinridge, Fargo felt on parade. Men poured out onto the main street to see Amelia sitting up on her sidesaddle with her petticoats billowing her skirts. Her bonnet was tied at a jaunty angle, her smile was firmly fixed, and she twirled a parasol while nodding and waving at her admirers.

Fargo had half-hoped that Amelia would have given up on roughing it by now, and wait somewhere, but Amelia had peculiar notions about wilderness travel. Odin, her big bay Tennessee walker, should have been swaybacked by now with the load she had on him. In her saddlebags and panniers, she'd brought everything but the kitchen sink, and she came close to that with a galvanized tub big enough for a footbath.

Not that Fargo had ever seen her use it—Amelia walled off the wilderness as readily as she had divided his cabin—but she had, not so subtly, offered to lend it to Fargo after several dirty days on the trail.

She washed her laundry right along with the dishes every night, and she was ready for the trail every morning, smelling of perfumed soap as she bustled around in her fresh-cleaned and wind-dried petticoats. Fargo was surprised that she hadn't brought an iron, but he was fairly sure that if he mentioned the omission, she'd rustle one up.

They had ridden out of Idaho Springs up the steep wagon road that climbed past George Jackson's big strike on Chicago Creek, then across Squaw Pass under looming gray peaks. Then they joined the caravan of eager prospectors and cursing freighters who struggled to cross the Continental Divide at Georgia Pass, which dropped them down onto the headwaters of the Blue River and its tributaries.

Every gulch, even above timberline, had men working its gravels. Most spots remained so cold that the men had to haul in firewood to thaw the sands before they could be worked with sluice boxes and rockers. By the time they got to Breckinridge, in the middle of all this mining excitement, he and Amelia had been an attraction for two days as miners streamed down from their diggings to idle along the main trail and stare at her as she rode by.

Fargo wasn't sure he liked being the celebrity who traveled with the current legendary darling of the mining districts. But leaving Amelia behind seemed futile, since she was so popular now that she could just snap her fingers and see a line of men who'd be proud to escort her as she followed Fargo.

Fargo felt nothing but relief as they left the mining camps behind and proceeded down the Blue. Having drawn up to not much more than shouting distance from the Southerners, Fargo slowed his pace, which gave Amelia the opportunity to spend her afternoons airing and washing everything within reach—including his shirts, pants, and buckskins, if he wasn't careful.

Uncomfortably aware of the lilac scent on his clothes, Fargo sat just above timberline on a barren windswept slope of scree, talus, and similar raw material for rock slides. He had no trouble identifying Arbuthnot, Smith, and Dexeter as the three men camped two thousand feet below him.

Their heavy wagon sat about a hundred yards away from the rushing river, which was still covered with ice in its quieter spots. Just on the other side of the wagon, they were going about their evening chores. Dexeter had to be the one tending the mules, Smith was setting up a canvas wall tent, and Arbuthnot was throwing some wood he'd just cut onto the fire. Across the river, the sun appeared to be balanced atop one on the spires of the jagged Gore Range that marked the west side of the valley.

Fargo's perch on the opposite side was in a string of mountains as yet undignified with a name, but they separated the Blue from the Williams Fork. Both rivers ran north to join the Grand in a broad mountain-rimmed expanse that they were now calling Middle Park.

Moving gingerly, to avoid starting a rock slide that would call attention to himself, Fargo worked his way down the slope. After every dozen or so catlike steps, he hunkered down and examined their camp. Dinner was almost ready—he could smell that their elk steaks were already too done to suit him—and the three Southerners sat around the fire, shifting to avoid the smoke that twisted every which way. Their conversation didn't carry as well as the aromas, though. Fargo could tell they were talking, and even which one was talking, but he couldn't make out distinct words.

Since he wanted to hear what they were saying to one another, he continued easing his way down the slope. Moving got easier the farther he went. Once in the shadow of the Gore Range, he didn't have to worry so much about being spotted, and the rock-strewn surface wasn't quite so steep. Higher up, every damned chunk of scree was perched at its precise angle of repose, ready to clatter downward with the slightest provocation. Down here, the rocks were sitting more comfortably, and so was Fargo as the men's drawls could be heard above the river's drone.

The Southerners were just complaining about Arbuthnot's cooking, as well as the slow pace of travel in these godforsaken mountains toward a destination they hadn't mentioned.

Fargo knew damn well where they planned to go, and he had known ever since Idaho Springs. Once he had realized that Middle Park was the same as Old Park, it had all fallen into place. The Southerners wanted to enlist the Utes, and they were traveling into the mountains.

This time of year, the Yamparika Utes always camped along the Grand River at some well-known hot springs that steamed and stank of brimstone, but felt good on aching muscles. The Utes sometimes took sore horses into the bigger natural-rock pools and let them wallow around for a while.

Dexeter, he noticed, was taking no part in the conversation—the painter was sitting off to the side, gazing at the summits afire with alpenglow, a reddish tinge that appeared when the sun was so low that only the very tips of the mountains caught its light. Was he thinking about his art? Fargo wondered. Or was he wondering about Amelia? When he wasn't coughing, which he seemed to do pretty regularly, Dexeter had that wistful look of a man who feels out of place.

Amelia, as best as Fargo knew, was camped about five miles upstream. After they'd set up, he'd told her he had to ride ahead and scout by himself. The notion of being by herself hadn't bothered her all that much—she said she could use a whole day of resting and washing—provided he'd promise to be back the next day. Fargo had promised, although he wasn't looking forward to fresh-scrubbed rocks and trees, and those had to be the only things around that Amelia hadn't already washed.

Following days of steady work in high altitudes, the Ovaro had stayed behind, too. The kind of work the Trailsman was doing this afternoon and evening, stalking about on rocky slopes, was best done on foot anyway.

After what seemed like years, Arbuthnot and Smith finally got around to talking about something more interesting than mud.

"How much longer do you think it will be before we get to the Ute camp?" Smith leaned back against a saddle and fetched a cigar out of his pocket, lighting it with a twig he pulled from the fire.

"Six, eight days, maybe more. Within two weeks, certainly," Arbuthnot replied, his bushy brows rising and falling with his voice. "As you might have noticed, it's quite difficult to follow a timetable with a team and wagon." He motioned to Dexeter. "And we've got other delays, too. Steve has to draw his pictures, and that takes some time."

Smith blew a smoke ring back toward the fire. "That's for sure," he drawled. "Well, I'll be glad when we get to the Utes. My blood seems a little thin for this godawful cold climate." As if to emphasize that, he shivered before continuing. "The only problem I can see is that goddamn Fargo, and you figure you've got his clock stopped, right?"

Arbuthnot allowed himself a toothy smile. "By this time tomorrow, he'll be deader than abolition. He's camped just a few miles behind us, and that's all the farther he'll ever go—in this life, anyway."

Fargo couldn't help but feel curious as to their plans for his short future, but their conversation shifted again as Dexeter leaned forward.

"When I was sketching some of the placer works along the Swan River," Dexeter said, "I heard about this Fargo character. They said he was traveling with a woman. That's unusual for a hired killer, isn't it?"

"Steve, everything about those professional gunmen is strange," Smith answered. "I don't know who hired that son of a bitch to track us and try to gun us down. Maybe it's someone trying to jump my and Arbuthnot's claims. Or it could be he's a bounty-hunter and he thinks one of us looks like somebody there's a reward for."

Fargo knew there were no claims. A little nosing around in Idaho Springs and Breckinridge had told him that. Smith and Arbuthnot had a few out, but they'd let them revert by not proving up on them. The claims were just a cover for their real purpose, but apparently Dexeter didn't know that.

"I don't like it," Dexeter said lowly. "You gentlemen haven't seen fit to discuss the details of your plans with me, but you should remember I'm funding this expedition. This Fargo is not alone; he is with a woman. I do not sanction gunfighters, but your plans of violent retaliation seem little better."

"Dammit, Dexeter. You've got to learn the ways of the West. Fargo and that woman you heard of might be working together—if she's any kind of looker, she could be the bait for some trap he sets," Smith asserted. "But I wouldn't pay no more mind to it. The senator has arranged for Fargo to start tracking in hell soon. That's the way it is, Steve. It's better than having him shooting at us."

Fargo wished he had been shooting at Smith, because he wouldn't have missed. But he sure couldn't remember having done so. Down below, Dexeter was quiet, brooding. The precise arrangements for Fargo's upcoming trip to hell would not be discussed, Fargo realized, but he knew now that Stephen Dexeter was not part of their plot. The artist was just a cover, like their earlier story that they were prospectors. It gave them an innocent explanation for their murderous mission.

Just how murderous their mission was became apparent to Fargo after the three men had gone to sleep, apparently so untroubled that they didn't bother to take turns on sentry duty. The Trailsman rose from his listening post in the boulders and stretched, grateful for the release. When he felt the tingle of blood circulating in his neglected legs, he crept toward the high-sided wagon. Once at its side, he carefully pulled himself up for a view of the bed and its contents.

Such light as the stars provided gave Fargo a fair idea of the contents: tins of sugar and coffee, sacks of flour, small kegs of powder and shot. None of that much bothered Fargo. Indians had to eat, too, and though some folks didn't think Indians should have guns or ammunition, there were so many people in the mountains these days that the game was all too spooked to hunt with the traditional bow and arrow.

It was the four bigger kegs just behind the seat that Fargo found most interesting. He leaned over and sniffed them to confirm his guess.

Whiskey. Or what they called whiskey, anyway. Definitely high-proof alcohol, and bound for the Utes, who would cheerfully kill for the stuff and just as cheerfully kill one another and anything else that was handy once they'd gotten into it.

First things first, Fargo thought. Get rid of the rotgut whiskey, and then deal with Arbuthnot and Smith. He couldn't quite see gunning them as they slept, although he was sure it wouldn't bother them a bit to do that to him. Besides, Fargo had to let Smith and Arbuthnot stay around long enough to tell him of their plans. If there were others involved, Fargo was going to know about it.

Dexter might be enough of a fool to let the Southerners keep their plots to themselves, but Fargo wasn't about to be that stupid. He suspected it wasn't going to be easy to get them talking. But he'd worry about that after disposing of the kegs.

As he slid the fourth and last keg back, edging it along so that any scraping noise was muffled by the sounds of the river, Fargo kind of wished he was an Apache. For one thing, they were trained from birth to be sneaky, and it was something he had to think about as he did it. He was good at it, but it sure wasn't natural for a man who liked to take big steps.

An Apache would get to count coup or otherwise improve his standing if he succeeded in sneaking undetected into an enemy's camp and making off with goods. As it was, Fargo was just getting a backache. Each keg held eight gallons and weighed close to seventy-five pounds. They were heavy enough so that moving sneaky with them was troublesome. Besides that, he'd damn near woke up the camp on the first keg.

Getting it out hadn't caused any problems, nor had carrying it on his shoulder while he walked slowly across the meadow, to a boulder-sheltered spot next to the creek where he could pop the bunghole with a rock so that the red-eye would trickle into the sand. Fargo figured he ought to at least know what he was pouring out, so he'd bent over and taken a swig as the liquid bubbled out of the tipped barrel.

The moment the substance hit his taste buds, he wanted to

cough and spit it out, and then maybe jump down and drink up the icy river. The liquor tasted worse than Taos Lightning, which generally stuck to soap and black pepper for flavorings. Much of the fire in this firewater came from the flaming red peppers they grew farther on down in New Mexico, and it was all Fargo could do to keep his mouth shut and stand quiet while the vile stuff tried to burn holes in his tongue and lips.

As he slid out the fourth and last keg, one of the mules spooked and started braying. That was the trouble with animals. You could pretty well tell whether men were asleep or alert, but at night, mules, donkeys, horses, and the like just stood there the same no matter how much attention they were paying to their surroundings. Fargo figured his best course was to grab the keg and get the hell out of there, but when he straightened with it, ready to step down from the wagon, Julius Arbuthnot came roaring out of the tent, wearing red wool flap-drawer long johns and toting a big Dragoon pistol.

Fargo was not going to let go of the keg and grab his Colt when the man already had the drop on him, so he let out the loudest "Hey, yaw!" yell he could summon. The startled Arbuthnot looked up and saw what had to be a marauding Indian stealing whiskey out of his wagon. A giant Indian at that, who raised the keg from his chest to over his head, and heaved it straight at Arbuthnot before the man could bring up his pistol.

Like a tenpin hit by a bowling ball, the senator sprawled back toward the tent, backing into a guy rope that buckled his knees and sent him into the canvas. The keg, after bouncing off Arbuthnot's belly, rolled along the ground behind him, and it arrived at the tent door, going in, at the same time as Smith, who had been fixing to go out, tripped on the keg and landed with his head atop Arbuthnot's belly.

Waving his arms frantically to clear himself of Smith and the ropes, Arbuthnot pulled the trigger just as Dexeter, lying low as the tent started to fall in around him, peeked out the door. Given the powder flash, the smoke, and the general darkness, Fargo couldn't tell much more of what was going on. Colt in hand, he leapt off the far side of the wagon and heard three voices cussing one another. Then the shots started coming his way, too fast for just one gun.

Much as he wanted to stop and fire back toward the camp, Fargo knew it wasn't the right time. Half-hoping that Smith or Arbuthnot would follow him, Fargo headed back upriver, toward the spot in the trees where he had stashed a few possibles after leaving his own camp that afternoon. It was just prudent to make sure some gear was handy when you were out afoot and didn't want to carry any more than you had to. It also made sense to cache those possibles where he could fetch them without leading any pursuers back to Amelia's camp.

Through what was left of the chilly night, Fargo stayed warm enough in the two blankets, but he didn't get enough sleep to matter. Apparently the Southerners had decided to reassemble their camp, rather than chase after whiskey-thieving Indians, but he couldn't be so sure that he'd relax his rest-robbing vigilance.

Mindful of what he had overheard about their plans to make this day his last, Fargo approached Amelia's campsite warily, circling the area and stopping to check on the hobbled Ovaro. Nothing seemed amiss until he got to camp, after both the sun and Amelia had been up and about their business for several hours.

At least he thought it was the camp he had left. The landmarks were right, but the place had changed. On the red-barked spruce trees that rimmed their clearing, Amelia had strung rope, which was now festooned with ruffled petticoats, billowing skirts, lacy chemises, and in general, more kinds of female clothes than Fargo knew how to name.

"Oh, Mr. Fargo," she chirped as he peeked through and felt some silken underthings slither about his ears. She straightened from the small tub of soapy water that sat, more or less level, on three rocks around the firepit. "I was most distressed about your welfare."

Fargo pushed on through and stood up. "So you decided to open up a laundry? Or is it a fancy-works shop?"

She stepped back, mistaking his hoarse tone of tiredness for anger. "Oh, no, Mr. Fargo. But I did hear gunplay last night."

"You slept close to your derringer, didn't you, honey?" Fargo looked around for something to sit on, and the ground looked as comfortable as anything. He got settled with his back against a tree and his legs sprawled out before him.

"Certainly," she replied, kneeling next to her washtub. "But I was still fearful. When I was a little girl, though, my mother told me that the best thing to do when one is fretful is to stay busy, instead of just pacing the floor or sitting there and imagining.''

"Sounds like your mother was a wise lady," Fargo replied. "What your imagination conjures up is usually a lot worse than what really happened."

"You're back," she murmured, dropping the satin blouse back into the washtub before she walked over and sat down next to him. "So whatever happened could not have been truly terrible." She wrinkled her nose and caught the sharp aroma of the rotgut over the soap smell. "Or was it? I thought we were away from the mining camps and their saloons, and yet you come back to camp reeking of the demon rum." She sidled away, finding her own tree to sit against.

Fargo didn't bother even trying to explain that he'd been destroying that whiskey, not drinking it. "I had a drink or two in a camp I ran across," he confessed.

Amelia didn't have anything handy to sew or wash, so she just had to get flustered for a minute or two, until with a little effort she managed to get her feathers adequately ruffled. "Mr. Fargo, you should remember you are in my employ," she stated imperiously. "I will not tolerate tippling."

"Really, Miss Parmeter?" Fargo asked dispassionately.

One chunk of bark seemed intent on boring into Fargo's back, so he stood up and stretched. Without even glancing at Amelia again, Fargo went over and started to roll up his bedroll.

"What are you doing, sir?" Amelia demanded, scampering to her feet and hurrying over to confront him as he hefted the bedroll to his shoulder.

"Leaving," Fargo answered. "I drink what I want, when I want to. So it seems I am no longer in your employ."

"But you can't leave," she gasped, following Fargo as she stalked toward the pinto.

"Can't I?" he asked, raising a questioning brow as he turned toward her.

"But you can't just leave me here," she whispered. "What will I do?"

"I've no idea," Fargo answered blithely as he fiddled with his saddlebags, trying to hide any amusement that showed in his lake-blue eyes from Amelia. "I suppose you've done all your laundry.''

"Oh, please, Mr. Fargo. Don't do this. Don't go."

"All right," he agreed readily. Fargo turned around and glared down at Amelia. He felt more like laughing, but the woman was getting mighty dictatorial and she needed to be set in her place. "I'll stay, providing you can remember that you hired me to find Stephen—not to roll over and sit up on command like some puppy."

Actually, Amelia hadn't been that bad. She had surprised him by being the kind of dreamy-eyed nature lover who smiled over every unusual rock and tree when she wasn't crouching beside the trail sniffing every new flower. Amelia had a way of cluttering up a campsite, but since she didn't complain too often, even though she was obviously accustomed to fewer chores and more amenities, Fargo felt her bizarre ideas of camping weren't worth commenting on.

But Amelia had been getting kind of impatient lately. More and more often, she'd been pretty moody, not bitching or anything, but pouting a lot. At night she had been no better company than a ground squirrel—nibbling at her food and not even bothering to say anything. And during the last few days she'd ridden along as if she were in a trance.

Fargo couldn't blame her. It was probably downright nerve-racking to be a pregnant woman getting closer and closer to a confrontation with a wandering lover. But Fargo wasn't about to let Amelia vent her emotional upsets on him, either—even if he did feel almost guilty about not telling her he had seen Dexter. But Amelia sure as hell didn't look pregnant, Fargo reflected as he stood there, still trying to glare at her, but knowing the glare had turned into a kind of appreciative inspection that wasn't nearly as safe.

Amelia Parmeter was the tiniest woman he had come across in a long time, with a waist he could easily span with his two hands. Fargo wished the pregnancy would start filling her out, because that might discourage him from measuring her—when she stood too close it was real hard not to put his hands on that tiny waist and pull her closer.

But Amelia Parmeter had a fiancé. And more than anyone, Fargo was hoping for an eventual happy reunion, because it would sure make his job a lot easier if Dexter was ready and willing to take Amelia off his hands. Then Fargo could send them on their way together, and the two of them, both Stephen and Amelia, would be out of range when the shooting started. The plan sounded too good to be true, and it just might be if Fargo didn't stay out of it. Sometimes, when Amelia looked at him, he didn't think it would take too much persuading to get her to forget Dexeter for a while.

Stepping back toward the tent, Fargo reminded himself that he didn't want Amelia to forget Dexeter. He wanted her to be as sweet and loving as possible when she was reunited with her beau. Fargo sure as hell didn't want Amelia making eyes at him in front of Dexeter, or even worse, making maudlin confessions of infidelity and begging for forgiveness. It was best to avoid that risk altogether.

At least, usually it seemed best. At the moment, Fargo thought it might be better to trust Amelia to use her head. After all, she was pregnant; she needed Dexeter. She might be persuaded to do something to warm a cold night, but surely she wouldn't do anything to ruin her future.

Even though Amelia tried to be prim and proper, there were times when she didn't act so aloof. It would be nice, Fargo thought. She'd like it. He knew he'd like it. And Dexeter would never know the difference. And then Fargo realized he was still just standing there staring at her.

"I shall prepare our luncheon," Amelia announced abruptly, looking up at him quizzically. "After we dine, my things should be dry. I'll repack and we can proceed."

"Sounds fair enough," Fargo agreed, suddenly remembering that the Southerners planned his demise for today.

If Amelia hadn't had every tree and bush covered with unmentionables, he would have packed up and gotten out of there as soon as he had gotten back. But women had a way of being difficult and unpredictable—too damned unpredictable for him to trust one to do the logical thing.

Obviously, the logical thing for Amelia to do was to greet Dexeter with open arms, then cozy up and overwhelm the man—like she overwhelmed every other damned thing including horses, trees, bushes, and prospectors.

While his eyes rested on a hodgepodge of drawers and chemises, Fargo decided that this afternoon, he and Amelia would get out of this place and go farther back in the woods where it would be more difficult to approach without noise. Then tomorrow, he would go steal Dexeter away from his companions. It wasn't safe for Dexeter to be with Arbuthnot and Smith much longer anyway, not with Dexeter being so damnably naive and ignorant that he would believe most anything those two bastards told him.

Amelia turned away, looking a little flustered as she went back to finish her laundry. Not quite able to clear his head of what might have been, Fargo watched as she fished something lacy and soapy out of the washtub. Amelia was one hell of a looker, the kind who could rope and hogtie most any man willing to settle down, and a few who weren't. And Fargo couldn't help but wonder what the woman had seen in Dexter.

Not that Fargo had really seen Dexter, not close up or full face, but he sure didn't have much admiration for the man. For a moment, Fargo wondered if he was jealous. But he wasn't. He was just naturally reluctant to pass up Amelia for the sake of someone who was too stupid to keep himself out of trouble. The truth was, if Amelia was smart, there was no reason to bypass anything. Dexter would never suspect.

"Do you need any help with those?" Fargo asked, waving his arm toward some laundry that looked to be dry and ready for packing. As it happened, his motion indicated several pairs of bloomers rather than the less interesting skirts.

A crimson blush spread across her face as Amelia stammered, "Oh, no, Mr. Fargo. You've already done enough today, I'm sure."

He grinned, knowing that she'd be even more embarrassed if he helped her pack her underthings and suchlike. He couldn't help but remember what a few glasses of wine did to wipe out her prudery. Fargo wasn't at all sure he liked the way his thoughts were running this morning. Amelia looked good, but she wasn't always all that easy to talk into things.

No, he realized. Talking her into things wasn't the problem. Talking her out of things was impossible. Against his protests, she had taken his cabin and slept in his bed, and now she was here when he didn't want her to be.

"Mr. Fargo, there are some things I should prefer to do without your supervision."

"You mean you'd like me to go for a walk?"

"Yes," she announced firmly. "I would like that. But luncheon will be ready when you return at noon."

Fargo checked the area around the campsite thoroughly before he saddled the Ovaro for a short trip down the Blue. Whatever the Southerners planned, there was, as yet, no one lurking in the brush. Downstream, as he had expected, Smith, Arbuthnot, and Dexeter had broken camp; he could spot the tracks of their wagon proceeding on down the valley.

There wasn't any point in shading them now, so he explored a few of the draws that led off the Gore Range. While he rode, Fargo made plans to rescue Stephen the next day. In some ways it would be better to let Stephen amble along with the Southerners a while longer. Finding Dexeter missing was probably going to spur Arbuthnot and Smith to action, and maybe that would limit Fargo's chances of really finding out who, if anyone, was behind everything.

But there was Dexeter to think of, and the man probably wasn't too safe where he was. And there was Amelia to think of. And considering that she was a modestly blushing, pregnant, soon-to-be-bride, Fargo was thinking on her all too much. Thus, Fargo pieced together a plan that would allow him to nab Dexeter with the least amount of risk.

When Fargo returned to camp, Amelia had been as good as her word. She had said "luncheon" and "dine," and that's just what she had spread out in the grass and gravel before the tent—a white linen tablecloth, complete with real shining silver knives, forks, and spoons. Even Amelia Parmeter wouldn't dare travel with china and crystal.

But somewhere in her bags she'd brought enamelware cups and plates, as well as two tins of oysters that made one fine pot of soup. The woman was actually learning how to cook, Fargo thought, and she served up better fare than any grizzled old trail hand. She even produced a pint-sized bottle of French wine, although Fargo kind of wished she'd left that hidden because it started his ideas churning all over again.

When Fargo marveled at her ability to civilize the wilderness, Amelia simply smiled. "It's more your doing than mine, sir."

"How's that?" Fargo kind of enjoyed the feel of a linen napkin against his face.

"You packed everything important, the necessities," she responded. "So I could bring these, shall we say, luxuries." Amelia continued, but Fargo comprehended little of it; along with her soft voice and the rustling of her laundry in the mild breeze, his ears caught harsher sounds—a snapping twig, boots squashing soggy leaves, metallic clatters.

In one smooth motion, Fargo grabbed Amelia and pulled

her down atop him. Wide-eyed, she looked down into his face. "Why, Mr. Fargo," she exhaled, "what has possessed you?" Ignoring certain signals from his loins, Fargo pulled her tighter. Her body didn't object, but her questions persisted. "Mr. Fargo, what are you doing? Why are you . . . ?"

A fusillade of bullets penetrated the row of fluttering petticoats and whistled across the campsite. Fargo released his grip and Amelia rolled off him, pressing as flat as she could against the pine needles and pointed gravel that carpeted the clearing. While Fargo rolled off his back and onto his belly, bringing up the big Colt before him, another thundering round of bullets put a second set of holes in Amelia's laundry. She looked there, then at him, but before she could ask another damn-fool question, they heard a sustained shrill yell from the other side of the petticoats.

Something like a cross between a mountaineer's yodel and a cat with its foot stuck in a trap, the chorus mystified Fargo. "What the hell is that noise?" he whispered to Amelia.

"The boys back home yell that way when they go hunting," she answered dazedly as the screeching built until it was enough to cloud anyone's wits. "Mr. Fargo," she whispered in awe, "I think they're hunting us." Any remaining doubts were erased by more gunfire and the sounds of at least half a dozen approaching men.

"Who's hunting us?" Amelia asked, her breaths coming heavy.

"Don't know," Fargo confessed. "Not Indians. They make too much noise. Sounds like there's six or eight of them thrashing around, happy like they treed a coon or something."

The clearing worked fine for a campsite and laundry room, but had serious shortcomings as a fort. Fargo couldn't see a damn thing that was happening out in the woods. A ruffled petticoat rustled over to Fargo's right. He twisted, bringing the Colt around to see a skinny kid in a checkered flannel shirt and blue jeans who hadn't started shaving regularly. Even so, the kid was big enough to hold a pistol until Fargo shot it out of his hand.

The kid yelped and turned tail. Responding to noises at his left, Fargo levered around and saw three youths crashing through the skirts. "Unhand her, you dastard," the tallest one shouted, his pistol shaking as much as his voice. All that Fargo had his hands on was his Colt, and he let one of the kids know that as his first slug shattered a boy's kneecap and the second punctured a youthful shoulder.

This bizarre teenaged army was falling back, perhaps to regroup, unaware of their good fortune. Fargo had been shooting only to maim the high-spirited youngsters. Some of these pups, he glumly thought, aren't ever going to walk straight again, but they ought to have considered that before setting out on this damn-fool hunting trip.

Then two more popped up. Fargo rolled around to discourage them, finding his arms atop Amelia's frozen back as he shot twice. Thanks to the smoke, the flutter of laundry, and mostly Amelia's sudden tensing, he missed both times, but the bullets came close enough to send the boys running.

With no time to reload the pistol, Fargo heard that yell again, along with some thrashing over to the side, and crawfished away from Amelia, going for his loaded Sharps. He arrived just in time to see a youngster race under the clothesline, waving a yard-long cavalry saber as he charged toward Fargo.

From his crouch, Fargo grabbed the barrel and jammed the stock up into the boy's rib cage. As the kid reeled back, Fargo got on his feet and brought up the Sharps in time to block an attempted saber slash.

At such close quarters, the Sharps worked better as a quarterstaff than as a rifle in this one-on-one combat. Although puffing from the belly blow, the kid moved lightly on his feet as Fargo met sword thrusts with parries, forcing the boy back, step by step, the shining saber ever in motion.

Almost at the clearing's edge, the boy jumped back. Grabbing the stock with both hands, Fargo knew he could club the kid to the ground. As he brought the rifle around, the kid's saber flashed high, catching and cutting Amelia's clothesline. The first petticoat slid down and blocked the saber. The kid looked up, surprised, in time to see an avalanche of ruffles and lace cascading his way. He started to turn and got tangled in the rope, followed by a pile of laundry that wrapped itself around him more tightly as he twisted.

Without time to laugh at the spectacle, Fargo turned to see the two boys he'd missed kneeling by Amelia, each with an arm, fixing to drag her off. She was still breathing, he could tell—in fact, she was seething with rage.

"Come on, Miss Parmeter, we've done rescued you. Hurry,"

one of them was urging her as the other tugged. Unaware that Fargo's Sharps was pointed at his head, he continued. "Please get up, ma'am. We've got to get you away from that kidnapper afore he spots us."

Amelia wiggled out of their grip and sat up. "I have not been kidnapped." She stood, shaking off the pine needles as the boys stepped back. "The man you saw here is my employee. I engaged him to—well, young man, why I hired Mr. Fargo, that is none of your concern."

The boys looked over to see the Sharps, its barrel looming big enough to crawl down. Their faces paled as the talkative one turned to Fargo. "But we was told that she'd been kidnapped by ah, er, uh, one of them white slavers that was gonna, er, well . . . ." He ran out of words that he could use in front of a lady, and the other stood speechless, so Fargo returned to the writhing mass of taffeta ruffles at the clearing's edge.

The saber waved until Fargo kicked it out of the boy's hand. Fargo knelt, his knee pinning the struggling form as he ripped off several layers of flounce to see a thin-faced sandy-haired youngster gasping for breath.

"You, sir, are no gentleman," the boy announced. Fargo stood, jerking the kid up with him.

"And you," Fargo told him, "don't look like much of any kind of man at all, let alone a gentleman." The kid tried to kick in response, but Fargo was out of range.

"What do you mean?" he stammered.

"I'm not the one all dolled up in petticoats," Fargo told him. "You squat to piss, too, you little whelp?" The kid glared as Fargo continued. "I'm going to be the one asking questions here. Just how much closer to manhood you get is entirely up to you."

The kid bent over, reaching for the saber with his constricted arm. Fargo halted his own kick when he saw the kid gingerly pick it up by the tip and straighten himself, presenting the sword hilt-first to Fargo. "We surrender, sir," he stammered. "Three of us is captured here, and you done took the other three out of the fight."

Fargo let the petticoat kid shuffle over to his companions, who sat shamefacedly under Amelia's glare. Fargo stepped over and stood next to her, looking down into her glistening eyes. "Miss Parmeter," he asked, "could you see to the wounded while these boys answer some questions for me?"

Amelia nodded and scurried off, guided by whimpering sounds off in the woods. Fargo just stood there, his face an expressionless but ominous mask to the three youngsters who sat quivering before him.

Their chattered answers confirmed what Fargo had already suspected. Knowing he and Amelia were behind them— mountain roads seemed to carry gossip faster than they transported men or mules—Arbuthnot and Smith had chanced upon a group of proud Georgia boys in Breckinridge.

Amid the other bullshit stories they had told the boys was one about how this big, mean galoot on a pinto had kidnapped a pure flower of southern womanhood and planned to carry her off to San Francisco and sell her to a Chinese ship captain, who would put her in chains, starve her, and sell her in a port clear on the other side of the world. Her new owner would whip her whenever she didn't pleasure the long lines of men she'd have to service every night. It was a fate worse than death, sure enough, so the boys should try to rescue the lady unharmed, but even if she were killed in the struggle, they'd be doing her a favor.

"That's what they told us, Mr. Fargo, honest," the petticoat boy concluded. "They said they was after you, too. We'd get a cash reward if'n we could rescue the lady from the Yankee scoundrel, an' there was five hunnert dollars in gold waitin' for us if'n we could kill that kidnapper. So we chewed on the notion after we seen you-all go through town, an', well . . ."

"Say no more," Fargo told him. "You can find your hurt friends and head on home. Just leave your guns here. You pups are too damn young to be playing with guns." With mournful looks, the boys shuffled out of the clearing, pausing only to get one free of his taffeta straitjacket.

Goddamn that Arbuthnot and Smith, Fargo thought. They use any people they can find. They used Stephen Dexeter for a mask to hide their own schemes. They wanted to use the Arapaho, and they were fixing to use the Utes, at whatever cost in the horror of a general Indian war. Then they used these kids to get him out of the way, putting Amelia in jeopardy as well.

He heard her skirt rustling through the brush and saw her in the afternoon light. If he hadn't known better, he would have sworn she was one of the wounded, for blood was splattered across her blouse and skirt, even her face, and she looked as sad as he felt.

"How bad were those kids bunged up?" he asked.

"One is going to lose a finger, but his hand will still be useful," she told him. "The shoulder wound was only a flesh wound. I cleaned it and he should recover. The boy you shot in the leg will limp, but he will walk."

"I wish it hadn't had to be that way," Fargo told her. "But they didn't give me much choice."

"No, they did not," Amelia agreed.

Silently, Fargo sat, and Amelia came over, smiled tiredly, and sat next to him, leaning wordlessly on his broad shoulders.

The Trailsman could feel her gentle undulation with every breath while he sorted out the day's events. Smith and Arbuthnot might have enlisted some help to waylay him, Fargo knew, but they hadn't been sharing the Indian schemes with anybody but themselves.

After questioning every postal clerk along the way, Fargo was pretty sure Arbuthnot and Smith weren't sending messages back home. But it was too much to hope that Arbuthnot was the only fanatic involved. Unfortunately, that meant Fargo would have to bide his time a little longer. Right now, Smith and Arbuthnot knew exactly where Fargo and Amelia were, and first things came first. Fargo's first order of business was to get the hell out of there.

But the hills were alive with gossips. As long as he and Amelia were on the road, every miner and his mule would carry the story along to the Southerners. It made Dexeter's position more dangerous, too.

Fargo suspected Arbuthnot and Smith had to be shielding Dexeter from most of the trailside small talk that seemed as natural out here as fireside chats—just like he had been keeping Amelia out of like conversations. Fargo hadn't wanted her to know Stephen was just up the road a piece, and in all likelihood, Arbuthnot and Smith wouldn't have wanted Dexeter to find out too much about Fargo—or that it was Amelia Parmeter that the so-called gunman traveled with. As it was, Dexeter seemed to have picked up more gossip than they could be comfortable with.

Hearing a slight sniffling, Fargo looked down at Amelia. "Something wrong?" he asked.

"No," she whispered. "It's just that . . ." Amelia glanced up at Fargo with misty eyes. "I don't understand. What kind of men has Stephen become involved with?"

"Bad ones," Fargo answered succinctly.

Amelia nodded while her warm hand worked along his leg before finding a home atop his huge right hand. And Fargo found himself thinking of Stephen, too—of how much fun Stephen would be having in bed with this damsel, and how annoying it was going to be for himself to spend many more nights around Amelia while behaving himself.

But now that the Southerners had attacked and missed, they would be on their guard. There was no way he could watch Amelia and kidnap Stephen at the same time, unless he took her along. And that would be too damned dangerous.

As it was, Fargo couldn't even risk leaving her alone. Two men who didn't balk at encouraging the slaughter of white settlers probably wouldn't have too many qualms about dispatching Amelia if she seemed to pose a problem.

"Mr. Fargo," Amelia murmured, "I want to thank you for saving my life today."

"Yeah, honey," Fargo muttered. "Anytime." But he wished Amelia would quit looking at him as if she liked him. It was disrupting his thoughts.

Scowling as he turned away from her to study on more important matters, Fargo tried to remember a high pass nearby that he had once crossed. It would lead to just about where he needed to go now, and it would let him get up off the road and bypass the Southerners. It was doubtful Smith and Arbuthnot would be looking ahead of them for Fargo, but if he took the pass, that's where he could be, waiting.

Unfortunately, it had been a long time since he'd gone over it, and Fargo had been with hunters who knew the area then. Besides, he had been across it in the fall, and the route might well be blocked this early in the year.

As Fargo considered the possibility of taking the pass, he wished he didn't have a woman along. Her presence kept him from feeling good about the idea of confronting the Southerners or taking the pass. But Amelia was along, so Fargo settled back and tried to remember the trail.

After weighing the danger of avalanches, rock slides, deep

snow, and just plain getting lost, since landmarks changed over the course of time and the trail had never been well-marked or oft-used anyway, Fargo decided he'd rather trust Amelia's fate to nature than to Arbuthnot. The pass would certainly get them away from the gossip and the Southerners because there definitely wouldn't be any up there.

"Why don't you start cleaning this place up?" Fargo suggested, glancing around at the litter of pantalets and petticoats strewn about, while Amelia nestled a lot closer than she generally did. One thing was certain, this was not the time or the place for nestling.

"We're pulling out in half an hour," Fargo announced, thinking that if Arbuthnot and Smith had decided to launch a new attack as soon as they'd found out the last one had gone awry, it would take them at least until then to instruct and send reinforcements.

"We're leaving today?" Amelia gasped. "Before I have time to rewash my garments?"

Fargo grunted and decided that at least this was as good a time and place as any to take a quick nap. There was always the hope that when he woke up, Amelia would be gone.

## 7

The top of the pass was snowed in, covered by a field of snow no wider than two city blocks, but it was wide enough and deep enough to look mighty nigh impassable.

"Goddamn, double shit, damn," Fargo muttered under his breath while deliberately stepping into the snow. He took several more steps, and the Ovaro snorted behind him, pawing and sidestepping and wheezing in order to let his displeasure be known. "Damn it, I know it's not possible," Fargo blasted, turning on the horse. "But we're going across here anyway."

They had climbed high on the trail, far above timberline. Since dawn, Fargo and Amelia had been toiling up the mountainside; for more than an hour, they had been working their way across rolling alpine tundra. And Fargo would be damned before he would accept that he'd come all that way only to reach a snowfield that swept upslope toward a steep gray ridge of scree, negotiable by a man, maybe, but not a horse.

On the downhill side the snowfield broadened, dropped from the heights, then disappeared over the edge of the earth. This wasn't the first snow they had come upon that day, but it was the first to look like trouble. There was no way to go but forward or back, and neither looked good.

Scanning ahead, Fargo would have sworn they had reached the barrenest, bleakest, most inaccessible place in the world—if there hadn't been remote blue-gray peaks jutting up in every direction. He dug in his feet, swore, and took another few steps forward while the Ovaro shied, pranced, and snorted out his own version of cursing. Glancing back, Fargo caught sight of Amelia, standing ten or fifteen yards down the trail with the big bay behind her.

The bay was placid, not being smart enough to figure out that where the Ovaro went, he would be expected to follow.

Amelia just looked tiny, tiny compared to her mount, and even tinier in comparison to the mountains.

So far this morning, Amelia had been no trouble to have along. Actually, she had been so quiet that Fargo had almost forgotten she was around. But seeing her there reinforced his uncomfortable notion that he was crazy if he thought he could get himself, two horses, and a woman across an expanse of snow a snowshoe rabbit would have had trouble negotiating.

"Wait there," Fargo shouted.

Amelia nodded.

The snow was slick stuff, having melted in the sun and refrozen a dozen times until in many places the crust resembled the surface of a skating pond. Fargo picked his route carefully, heading uphill, away from a shimmering, slicker-looking patch. He had to stomp down hard to get a foothold in the snow, but the Ovaro broke right through the crust.

"You only think you're sinking," Fargo muttered, trying to keep the horse moving. "Why, there's at least eight or ten feet of this stuff under you. And you've only dropped eight or ten inches."

There was a kind of perverse pleasure in telling the horse something that would have horrified a man. But Fargo didn't get a similar pleasure out of knowing that at any minute, the heavy horse might actually sink several feet.

"Look," Fargo told the Ovaro. "You're the one got yourself into this fix. If you'd just walk straight, you wouldn't sink more than six inches. It's all this stomping around that's doing you in."

Fargo pushed and pulled and cajoled the pinto. Then he mounted, leaned far forward, and whispered endearments in the animal's ear as he tried to ride the Ovaro through the drift. He dismounted and tried bellowing obscenities.

"Would you rather be shot at?" Fargo demanded. "Go back down there and you'll have bullets flying at you. And that goes for the lady, too," Fargo warned, trying to appeal to the horse's finer sensibilities. "I sure as hell don't know why, but you seem to like her."

Fargo led the horse ahead several inches, let the animal back off, then jumped up and down on the trampled snow, feeling like an idiot as he tried to pack it down harder. Fargo leaned on the horse's backside, knowing that if ever his old friend was going to kick him to hell and back it would be now. And each technique gained him about six inches.

"Come on," Fargo muttered encouragingly. "You can trust me. You know I'll get you out. Even if you end up ear-deep in it."

Fargo sweated and the horse sweated, but the man stayed cool by landing with his own backside buried in snow at least a dozen times. Magnificent animal that he was, the Ovaro had nonetheless lost his nerve. Halfway across, the horse was near up to his ass in snow, and floundering. He was balking back like an old mule and giving Fargo that baleful, sad-eyed look only horses can muster. The dark-eyed terror of the Ovaro was a lot harder to resist than a woman's tears.

"All right," Fargo relented.

It wouldn't do him any good to get the pinto across only to find that the bay wouldn't abide being similarly tortured, anyway. Fargo soothed his horse, then went back to test his luck on the bay.

"You're on your own," Fargo told Amelia as he took her horses's lead from her. "You can rest here awhile, but when you come, keep your feet in my tracks."

The bay was hanging back before they even stepped foot in the snow. Groaning, Fargo hunched his shoulders and threw his weight into persuading the animal. Before too long, he felt as if he were building pyramids all by himself. The horses were no more cooperative than blocks of stone; they had to be nudged, nagged, sweet-talked, cursed, and finally dragged every inch of the way. Pouring sweat and aching miserably, Fargo paused, looked up, and was confounded to find he had actually made some progress. He had both horses well past the midway point.

Triumphantly, he glanced back to see what Amelia thought of it all. But Amelia wasn't anywhere nearby. She had walked back down the trail a ways and was sitting on a boulder gazing off in the other direction. "Sightseeing again," Fargo muttered.

But at least the horses had given up on resisting. They didn't help, but they didn't hinder, either. They had quit backing off six inches for every foot taken, and as Fargo paused to rest again, he could actually see his way through.

He had reached the far side of the ice field. The snow in front of him sloped down toward the trail. And the snow beneath him probably wasn't more than five feet deep. It was a relief to know it was no longer possible to lose a whole horse in it.

While stretching his own weary muscles, Fargo paused to soothe and pat both horses, mumbling about what good boys they had been when in actuality they'd been as stubborn as any ten jackasses.

Amelia's scream pierced the air, and the Ovaro's head jerked up, pushing Fargo backward. The Trailsman scrambled up and scanned the ice field where Amelia was sliding and gaining speed like a runaway sled.

"Quit flaying," Fargo hollered. "Kick in your heels hard."

Amelia brought up her legs and kicked down hard, but she didn't make any impression on the crusted ice. She tried again and the action pitched her sideways, slowing her a little.

The slope beneath her leveled off, just a bit, but it was enough. Amelia kicked in a minor foothold. With one boot dug in to give her some friction, she slipped another foot or two before coming to a precarious stop.

Stretched out on the snow with her arms over her head, Amelia started to claw at the ice with her hands, but then she slipped another few inches. Obviously frightened, she froze up and lay unmoving, looking like a small discarded doll far down on the broad white field. She was just a smidgen of color and a slight restless movement as her rumpled skirt and petticoat caught the breeze.

"Stay still," Fargo boomed, and the words echoed back, sounding peculiar to his ears.

He only hoped she could stay still. It didn't really matter what he shouted at her, Fargo knew damned well that if the slope hadn't leveled out, nothing in the world could have saved Amelia. She'd been going too fast to help herself. And if she started gliding again, it was unlikely she would stop.

"You two stay here," Fargo ordered the horses. Presumably the command was unnecessary, but considering the circumstances, it would be just like those two to start moving now.

Grabbing the Sharps, Fargo headed back across the horse-trodden snow. When he got to where he was over Amelia, he started down on foot, but the surface was too slick, and it was all too likely he would fall on his ass, bypass Amelia, and sail on over the cliff himself. That sure wouldn't do her any good, and Fargo was fairly sure he wouldn't enjoy it much himself. Cursing, he eased down on his belly.

Creeping backward, Fargo had only gone a few yards when his foot slipped. Before he could get another toehold, he slid a good three feet. He hadn't built up much speed and he'd stayed pretty much in control, but the slip gave him a queasy notion of what it would be like to slide right over the edge of the world.

Gripping the Sharps tighter, Fargo got ready to slam it into the snow and use it as an ice ax if he had to. It seemed a poor way to treat a good gun, but then again, if Fargo pitched over the side of the mountain, so would the Sharps.

It was a long way down to where Amelia lay, and a considerable way back up. Above Amelia the icy slope swept upward; below her it swept down a bit more gently for perhaps a hundred yards before it disappeared. Whichever way Fargo viewed it, her position didn't look promising.

Peering down, Fargo could see that Amelia's eyes were squeezed tight and her fists were clenched. She looked scared, but he couldn't blame her, since her grasp on the mountain relied on a capricious fate and a two-inch toehold. He didn't like looking at her, so he didn't. Seeing her would only make him hurry, and hurrying could only land him in a worse spot than Amelia was in.

Patiently and carefully, Fargo inched his way down. It was funny that the snow didn't make him feel cold, but the sun was high and beating down, glaring off the white surface and making it even slicker. Finally, he was within arm's reach of Amelia. Fargo edged down until his face was even with hers before he kicked as safe a hold as he could in the icy surface.

Mentally apologizing to the trusty Sharps, Fargo lanced the rifle into the snow between them. "Amelia," he said, intending to tell her to take hold of the rifle.

Amelia opened panic-stricken eyes and immediately lunged for Fargo. Knowing her weight would unbalance him, Fargo threw his hand forward and grabbed the rifle butt, but Amelia missed him. Flipping onto her belly, she started to glide and shriek.

Instantaneously, Fargo twisted and thrust his foot between her legs. Throwing both arms around Fargo's thigh, Amelia wrested him toward her. For a moment, they were both hanging on to the mountain by one handhold. Amelia was still screaming as Fargo gingerly eased his free foot back onto his makeshift ledge.

It was a miracle the Sharps had held, since Fargo had never expected its placement in the ice to be so thoroughly tested. Between the horses and Amelia, it was turning into one hell of a day, and as Fargo listened to the echoes of Amelia's screams, he scanned the snowfield above him. Their chances of making it back looked pretty slim. But there was no use discouraging Amelia; she was going to need all the courage she could find.

Fargo reached down and took hold of her hand, drawing her up beside him. "Going somewhere, Miss Parmeter?" he asked wryly.

Amelia had lain on the snow unmoving for quite some time. Her hands were icy, her lips were blue, and her jaw was trembling. But Fargo could tell she was trying to build up her gumption. After several minutes she quit shivering against him and whispered, "I'm going wherever you take me, Mr. Fargo."

He could only hope that would be back to the trail. But there were no guarantees. The texture of the snow on the slope was changing and unpredictable. It could crumble beneath them, it could refuse to hold the Sharps, it could turn mushy and soft.

While Amelia did exactly what she was told, clinging to him whenever they stopped to rest, and looking at him as if he offered salvation, Fargo chopped steps in the ice. Fargo felt like telling the woman that this was no staircase to heaven; one mistake on his part, and it would most likely lead directly in the opposite direction.

While he used his knife to scrape out another step, making sure the ledge angled down into the snow so there would be no chance of sliding off, Amelia kept her arms around him and pressed herself against his side, distracting him. Never had she been so wholeheartedly agreeable. But there was no possible way for Fargo to take advantage of it.

Just as he suspected, Amelia was not nearly as friendly once he had her back on dry ground. She was grateful enough, stammering out apologies and thank-yous while she stood there, wringing her hands and glancing up at him as if he were an archangel or something—instead of a flesh-and-

133

blood man who would have appreciated a heartier display. Although seeing Amelia there in one piece made Fargo feel like celebrating, all her proclamations of undying gratitude only made him uncomfortable. He went back to see to the horses.

They had calmed considerably and Fargo had them out of the snow within the hour. The trail down the mountain was steep, but clear, and by midafternoon he had found a suitable campsite, a large clearing in a grove of aspen. High on the mountainside, it would be damned cold at night, but now the sun's warmth filtered down through trees just starting to bud.

The place was isolated, but it wasn't more than a mile or two above the wagon road that twisted along the Blue. From here, Fargo could easily scout the road for the Southerners. And the clearing was secluded; it would be a safe place to leave Amelia while he worked.

Satisfied with place, Fargo rolled out his bedroll in the sun and sprawled on top of it. He figured he deserved a siesta, but Amelia was bustling around rearranging the wilderness as if it needed a good spring cleaning. Fascinated, Fargo watched her move rocks and deadfall aside, fashion a table and cover it in while linen. Then, she stuffed blankets into green satin pillowcases and plumped them up to serve as chairs. She produced silver and plates and even candlesticks, although how she planned to keep the candles lit in the mountain breeze was beyond Fargo. Amelia had been disrupting nature all along the route, but her industry never ceased to amaze him.

"Why don't you settle down for a while?" Fargo suggested. "It's been a long day."

"But there's so much to do, sir," Amelia countered, not even glancing at him as she hung up her bedding to air.

There was no purpose in resting when Amelia was in one of her redecorating moods. Just watching her made him tired. If he was just going to get worn out anyway, Fargo figured he might as well do something. Resigned, he set himself to chopping wood.

Fargo retrieved some of the deadfall Amelia had cast aside, but he had no sooner lifted the ax than his shoulder felt as if the fires of hell had been lit within. It had ached ever since he had pushed the horses around. Now it throbbed with heat, and when he brought the ax down, it felt like someone had actually managed to run a saber through him.

Realizing he had probably sprained it, Fargo groaned, but there was no reason to give up on the wood. Sooner or later, they were going to need it. The ax stuck fast, and automatically Fargo yanked it loose.

A mule couldn't have kicked him harder than the pain. Swearing, Fargo tried to steady his injured shoulder with his other hand as he swung the ax back up, but the blade lanced sideways, tearing off a piece of bark. Fargo paused, waited for a racking spasm to pass, and raised the ax again.

"Mr. Fargo," Amelia said from behind him, but from so close it sounded as if she'd spit the words into his ear.

Fargo missed the wood entirely as the sweep of the ax barely missed his leg. He escaped slicing his leg, but it felt as if his shoulder had come unhinged. "Goddammit," Fargo thundered, whirling on Amelia. "Haven't you done enough today? If you were hoping to witness an amputation, I'm sorry I disappointed you, but I'm not that clumsy."

Looking as if she were going to cry, Amelia spun on her heel and sprinted toward the woods. The forest was choked with deadfall, floored with slippery rotting aspen leaves, and stubbled with rocky outcroppings, but Amelia hurtled through with her petticoats lifted high. Fargo halfheartedly chased after her, but she moved like an antelope.

Amelia left the aspen grove behind and wended between the evergreens. Tiny and fleet, she bounded right over fallen logs and protruding rocks. She came to a maze of fallen timber, but she merely ducked down and rolled between two twisted trunks.

Fargo couldn't accept that he was losing ground, but Amelia slipped right between tree trunks and deadfall Fargo had to skirt. He was too big for the kind of chase she was leading. A fallen ponderosa blocked Amelia's path, but instead of stopping, she dropped to her belly and squirmed beneath it. Chasing Amelia seemed as pointless as chasing a wild animal, and it occurred to Fargo that if he wanted to stop her, he'd have to shoot her.

Amelia veered and headed uphill, but she didn't seem to lose her wind. Fargo couldn't believe the delicate, southern beauty was still running, and she wasn't just running, she was stampeding as crazily as a spooked longhorn. He cursed when he saw the dense, gray stand of lodgepole ahead, their scrawny trunks growing close together.

The deadfall was treacherous. Amelia vaulted over, then scrambled under one spindly trunk after another. But finally her petticoats caught fast, held, then ripped, pitching her onto her belly.

Slowing, Fargo tried to catch his breath and cool his wrath before he got to Amelia. She could well be dead, but if she wasn't, he'd probably murder her.

She wasn't dead. With her knees drawn up under her skirts and her arms stretched out, she sprawled on her back, gasping for air. And Fargo realized immediately that she wasn't even hurt. Between breaths she was actually smiling, as if catapulting through the forest was an amusing pastime.

"Miss Parmeter," Fargo blasted, "if you think this race has improved my temper, you're sadly mistaken."

"Oh, Mr. Fargo," she gasped, sitting up hastily and staring at him as though she hadn't expected him to be there. She wrapped her arms around herself protectively as the color drained from her cheeks. "Oh," she whispered, "I am sorry."

Sighing, Fargo nodded and sank down onto the ground to rest against a tree trunk as he rubbed his shoulder. The pain had graciously begun to recede from a searing fire to a dull ache, but the race had jarred it enough to make him give up all hope that it would be better in the morning.

"You're hurt," Amelia blurted, scrambling over to his side. "Did you fall, sir? Or did you scrape it on a tree? Oh, Mr. Fargo, I am so sorry. And it's all my fault."

Fargo stared at her, not quite sure that a creature so contradictory could be real. Then, leaning his head back against the tree, he closed his eyes. Amelia actually looked sympathetic, an image that was just too difficult for him to contemplate, so he shut it out.

"I sprained my shoulder hauling the horses around," he admitted.

"Perhaps, if you took off your shirt I could tell if there was swelling," Amelia suggested.

Fargo opened his eyes and scowled at her suspiciously, but he complied. He tensed as Amelia bent over his shoulder, but her fingers only fluttered over his skin.

"It's swollen," she announced. "But I've some balm in my saddlebags."

"You've enough in your saddlebags to start up a mercantile," Fargo muttered.

"Well, perhaps," she admitted. "But it's best to be prepared, don't you think?"

"Yes," Fargo agreed as he stood up and put his shirt back on. "But tell me, Miss Parmeter. How does one prepare himself for you?" He started walking toward camp.

And Amelia followed. "You are teasing, aren't you?" she asked worriedly. "I honestly did not intend to upset you, sir."

"It just comes easy, right, honey?"

When Amelia didn't answer him, Fargo glanced around to be sure she hadn't bolted again, before deciding he wouldn't chase her even if she did. By his reckoning, they already had a good two miles to walk.

Back in camp, Fargo flung himself down on his bedroll, determined to catch the last warmth of the afternoon sun, while Amelia gathered what wood she could and made a fire. "I'll chop some later," he volunteered as she returned with another armload.

"Oh, no, sir," Amelia protested. She went over to her saddlebags and withdrew a bottle. "We have to take care of your shoulder."

Lazing in the sun wasn't proving too enjoyable since his shoulder had gone back to throbbing, so Fargo let Amelia try her balm. The stuff was gooey and cold, but her fingers were soothing.

"Feels good," Fargo admitted. "I guess men weren't meant to haul horses around," he added, mumbling to divert himself because his mind kept wandering to other things Amelia could do that would feel good. "I guess that's why it usually works the other way around."

Fargo waited, but Amelia didn't say anything. "I guess I'll give in to my curiosity," he conceded. "What in hell were you smiling about out there?"

"I don't know," Amelia answered. "I suppose sometimes it just feels good to be alive. And it felt that way, out there. But I am sorry," she apologized quickly, for perhaps the fiftieth time that day.

Fargo rolled over to look at her, and Amelia spread goo across the front of his shoulder, leaning across him to knead it into his sore muscles.

"That's good enough," Fargo muttered gruffly, resisting an urge to pull Amelia down on top of him.

Amelia sat back on her heels as Fargo sat up. "Does it hurt terribly?" she whispered. Her eyes swept across his bare chest and her color started to rise. "Would it be too much for me to expect you to finish what we began at the cabin?" she asked hesitantly.

"I'll find Dexeter for you," Fargo assured her.

Amelia raised her eyes and stared at Fargo's face, and she flushed before glancing away. "I didn't mean that," she mumbled. "I meant what happened the night we dined together." Amelia glanced back at Fargo before she sprang to her feet, looking as if she were going to run off again, although she went no farther than the fire.

"You're asking me to screw you?" Fargo blurted, and Amelia let out a little cry. "I'm sorry," he countered instantly. "I suppose there were better ways to put that. But you took me by surprise."

"That's quite all right, Mr. Fargo," Amelia answered, straightening her slim shoulders as she turned to face him.

She stood there, gathering her dignity, and Fargo realized he'd never seen her looking so disheveled. Her dress was dirty, her torn petticoat dragged, and there were pine needles in her hair. But she was certainly pretty enough. In the sunlight, her hair was as yellow as dandelions. For a moment her jaw quivered, but she steadied it.

"I'm not familiar with your phraseology, sir, but I believe that is what I am asking."

Fargo studied her warily, half-expecting her to fly back into the woods. Finally, he grinned. "My shoulder's improving rapidly," he commented. "You're a good nurse."

"What do I do now, sir?" she asked uncertainly.

"I think it's time you left that up to me," Fargo suggested.

Standing up, he approached Amelia cautiously. She seemed as skittish as a doe, but when he reached out for her, Amelia melted against him. Her eyes fluttered shut and her lips parted.

Knowing what she wanted, Fargo kissed her. But remembering how contrary she was, he didn't take any chances. His right hand moved directly to the buttons on the front of her dress. Without Aphrodite along, Amelia had taken to wearing more practical clothing, and Fargo had the dress undone before he let her come up for air. After he loosened the pins in Amelia's hair, it cascaded down cross her back and shoulders, making the elegant belle look tousled and wanton.

Underneath the dress, Amelia wore a chemise and pantalets and petticoats, but no corset. Fargo had known she couldn't be wearing the whalebone perversion she had worn before—it took two to manage it—but he had figured she'd be wearing something to cover her advancing pregnancy. Instead, he felt softly rounded curves beneath the linen.

There was a certain shyness in the way she didn't quite look at him as she stepped back to finish undressing, but she was considerably calmer than she had been earlier. Her petticoats dropped to the ground, followed by the pantalets, and Amelia reached down to pull the chemise up over her head.

Naked, Amelia was as near perfect as any woman Fargo had ever seen. Surprised, he reached out and ran his hand along the curve of her hip, and her belly was flat beneath his palm.

Fargo slipped his hand up across her soft, well-rounded breasts and almost laughed as Amelia swayed beneath his touch. With her breasts bared, her hair flowing, her eyes closed, and her cheeks rosy, Amelia looked more like his own romanticized notion of a mythical wood nymph than like a real woman.

But her reactions were earthy enough. Fargo slipped a hand between her thighs, and Amelia drew in a ragged breath and fell against him. "You sure as hell don't look pregnant," he murmured into her hair.

"What?" Amelia cried, pushing away from him.

Fargo realized his mistake instantly. Most so-called ladies considered a mention of pregnancy or anything else of a biological nature worse than cursing. "I suppose I shouldn't have mentioned that," he admitted, although the subject hadn't seemed to dampen her ardor that night at the cabin.

Mentally, Fargo cursed the society that had produced a whole gender whose sense of what was and wasn't proper defied rationality. On the other hand, even though he couldn't quite see how so many women got through the process without so much as mentioning it, pregnancy wasn't really his favorite subject either. He certainly didn't mind abandoning the topic.

"We'll just forget it. All right?" he suggested reasonably, stroking Amelia's hair.

But Amelia whirled away, not turning back until she was out of Fargo's reach. "What makes you think I'm . . . I'm . . . I . . ." she stammered, blanching as she realized how close she had come to mouthing an obscenity. "You know," she finished softly.

"Aren't you?" he asked.

"Good heavens, no," she bristled.

"But that's what you told me back at the cabin," he protested.

Amelia simply stared at Fargo for several minutes, apparently forgetting she was standing there in nothing but her stockings and high-topped boots. And Fargo stared back, watching her breasts rise and fall as she breathed.

"You didn't hear a word I said that night," she accused him.

"You weren't speaking real clearly," he objected, then shrugged. "And I'll admit my mind wasn't on what you were saying."

"Oh," she whispered, her anger dissipating with the sound.

Amelia's expression was one of incredulity, as if she thought Fargo as difficult to fathom as she was. He took a wary step forward, but Amelia stepped back. Shaking her head as if to clear it, she turned away.

And Fargo tensed, ready to give chase. After seeing her hurl through the forest encumbered by petticoats, he didn't even want to envision her fleeing through the bushes naked. He supposed it would be something to see, but just thinking on it made his shoulder ache.

Amelia shook and her long hair rippled. Drawing in a shuddering breath, she tossed her head back and the golden tendrils caressed her buttocks. Fargo thought she was crying, but Amelia glanced back and he realized she was laughing.

"How embarrassing," she spluttered. "As if I weren't embarrassed enough. Pregnant?" she gasped, twirling back around. "Pregnant? *Enceinte*, breeding, expectant, heavy with child," she tossed the words out gleefully. "Oh, Mr.Fargo . . ." She laughed. "Did you really think I would tell you such a thing?"

Fargo didn't need to answer, for Amelia whirled away

again and dropping down on a rock, started to take off her boots.

"And who, pray tell, did you think was the father of my child?" Tossing a boot aside, Amelia stared up at Fargo with brilliantly sparkling eyes. "Or did you think there were hordes of candidates?" She tossed her second boot aside and spluttered with laughter. "I suppose, considering the nature of your experiences with me, you probably concluded my gallant, young admirers were all off hiding in the swamps and piney woods. Am I right, Mr. Fargo?"

"Actually, I assumed Stephen Dexeter was the father," he answered.

"Oh," Amelia whispered, and her smile faltered. "That would be nice," she murmured. "But Stephen and I were always careful about such things. I assure you, sir, an heir before the wedding would be considered most inappropriate where I come from."

"I know that," Fargo chafed. "I figured that's why you were looking for Dexeter."

"I wish you were right," Amelia murmured. Then she gave Fargo a glorious smile. "Don't look so distraught, sir. You have done me a wondrous favor. Today, I've fallen off a mountain, run off to the woods, propositioned a gentleman, and been accused of being pregnant. I think I've passed my threshold of embarrassment, and I see no reason now to even try to behave correctly. Oh, dear, it tickles," she commented, looking down at her bare feet as she stood up.

Amelia skipped to the side, did a little two-step, and pretty soon she was dancing all over the clearing. If a jury had asked Fargo to attest to Amelia's sanity, he would have confessed he thought she was mad. But nonetheless he enjoyed her display.

Laughing giddily, Amelia spun faster and faster, oblivious to the sharp stones and twigs underfoot. Her hair whirled around her, catching the sunlight, and her pale ivory flesh shimmered as it turned and twisted beyond the golden swirl. Amelia stopped spinning, staggered dizzily, and dropped onto the bedroll.

She lay on her back, smiling and looking much as she had in the woods, except she was naked. Fargo sat down beside her without taking his eyes off her heaving breasts.

"Sometimes it just feels good to be young and healthy," Amelia murmured. "Does it not, sir?"

"Sure," Fargo agreed.

Amelia opened her eyes and looked at him questioningly. "Would you care to make it feel better?" she whispered.

She didn't have to ask twice. Nor did Fargo give her a chance to change her mind. Stripping off his pants, he joined her on the bedroll. He bent to taste a small pink nipple, but Amelia's fingers slid across his swollen organ and she tugged at his good shoulder.

"Please, Mr. Fargo, do it now," she whispered.

More than happy to please a lady, Fargo rolled on top of her and plunged in. Amelia gasped, threw her head back, and wrapped her arms and legs around him. Her breasts and belly rolled against Fargo and her lithe body snaked closer.

Slithering sinuously, Amelia burrowed her shoulders into his muscle as her hips wove from side to side and up and down. She pressed hard, bringing him in deep, then fell away before surging up again.

Fargo thrust back and she moaned. He thrust again and she shrieked. Taking his cue from her, he thrust harder and faster. Within seconds, Amelia was breathing faster than she had after a two-mile run. Her legs clasped tighter and her moist center undulated rhythmically.

Amelia roused quick and steady, with her muscles straining and her breathing building to something akin to the chugging of a steam engine. Fargo could feel her heart throbbing, its tempo matching the pulsing of her core. Rising up over her, he caught the flash of her hair shining in the sun, and he came down hard.

Amelia swept up to meet him. A tiny thing, almost fragile, but she was like a boiler under pressure. Deceptively strong, she pressed against him. On the outside she was still, but hot and tense, while her inner machinations clamored like gears and rods run amok. And then she blew, taking Fargo with her as she pitched into wild, unholy screeching.

Amelia settled slower than she built. The screeching stopped, but she wiggled and squirmed and stretched against him. Then she set to hugging and mewing and gliding her hands along his sides. It made Fargo think of staging an encore, but the breeze was cooling and the fire needed feeding. Reluctantly, he pulled away and got up.

"You are a marvel, Mr. Fargo," Amelia sighed, watching him as he tossed wood into the fire.

Fargo straightened, and he was almost glad he had left her, since the view was better from up high. But then Amelia shivered and crawled into his bedroll, tucking all her curvaceous beauty away. Abruptly, she sat up, clutching a blanket at her breast. "You don't mind if I borrow your bed, do you, sir?" she asked, looking genuinely concerned.

Remembering how they'd met, Fargo laughed. Then a more recent recollection seized him, and Fargo went back and slipped in beside her. "I never mind if a beautiful woman borrows my bed, honey," he told her, "as long as she's willing to share it."

Amelia snuggled close and rubbed up against him with skin as soft and smooth to the touch as talc. "I wanted to thank you," she whispered. "For this. And for saving my life today." While pressing her breasts to his side, she fingered the hair on his chest restlessly. "But I wanted you to know, sir . . ." She paused and sighed, squirming even closer before she continued. "I wanted you to understand that I truly do love . . ."

Amelia glanced up sharply before she fell into helpless giggles. Gasping for air, she wriggled up and propped herself on her elbow to look down on Fargo's face. And her fingers took to playing with the hair behind his ear.

"Oh, my, how you do tense up at those words," she teased. "Yet today you were like a knight rescuing the beleaguered princess. You saved me, Mr. Fargo, with no thought of the danger to yourself."

"I assure you," he interrupted, "I was pretty concerned about my own hide."

"Of course." She laughed. "And yet you risked it regardless. A man like you is the dream of every southern girl. Noble, able, courageous. Don't laugh, Mr. Fargo. I may be trifling with you, but I'm serious." Amelia smiled at him wistfully as her hand moved down to caress his injured shoulder. "You would be very easy to love, Skye Fargo. But I suspect you would find the consequences of that sentiment a burden."

Sighing, Amelia burrowed back under the covers. "You needn't worry," she whispered. "I was merely going to tell you that I love Stephen Dexeter. And that he's dying. It was what I was trying to tell you at the cabin.''

"I'm sorry," Fargo muttered, knowing the words were inadequate.

"You, sir?" she protested. "Oh, no, you, of all people, shouldn't be sorry. I've been so frightened. I've never been away from home before, and I've been most difficult and brooding, to say the least."

"You're not so bad," he mumbled, his hands resting on curves that were well worth a little trouble.

"But you were right," Amelia confided. "Stephen has no intention of returning to me. For months before he left, he refused to see anyone. He claimed he was behind in completing a commission for several paintings." Amelia tightened her embrace and Fargo could feel her shivering. "But I insisted. Stephen wasn't painting, he was abed. He was thin, coughing, flushed. His eyes were so bright," she breathed. "But he said it was only a cold."

"You sure it wasn't?"

"Dr. White told me Stephen has consumption," she confessed. "Of course, he revealed that professional secret only after I plagued him unmercifully."

"Maybe Stephen will get better."

"His case was far advanced, but Dr. White assured me consumption sometimes clears in the high, dry air of the West. But Stephen never said anything. He was very affectionate and he said he'd miss me. But he never even hinted he wouldn't be coming home." Amelia's voice sounded hollow and distant, but this time there was no whimpering, gasping, or crying to distort her meaning. "I suppose he thought I would be notified of his death after it happened; he probably thought he was being kinder that way."

"Maybe he plans to get better and go home."

"No," she whispered. "The climate is too damp. Stephen can never return home again. He'll never take up his place at Dexeter Plantation. Even if he does recover."

Her tears were hot on his shoulder, but Amelia was struggling for control, and Fargo murmured assurances and comforting words because he knew that was what she wanted. But he felt they were as irrelevant as the sweet talk he'd fed the horses earlier that day. The truth was, Dexeter could already be dead. If the consumption hadn't gotten him, the Southerners might well have.

"I believe Stephen loves me," Amelia asserted, her voice growing stronger. "I believe he's only trying to protect me. But I can't swear to you, Mr. Fargo, that he will be pleased to see me."

"We'll just have to wait and see. No sense worrying about it now."

Her chin rubbed against Fargo's chest as she nodded. "My parents knew about Stephen and me," she whispered. "They said he left because a gentleman doesn't marry an immoral woman. They might be right. But I don't care, Mr. Fargo. I love him. I have to see him to be sure he's all right."

"Sounds fair."

"If Stephen doesn't want me here, you'll take me back to Denver, won't you?"

"I'll see you get home."

"I can't go home. Jeffrey was most eager, but my parents, of course, did not approve of this journey. The scandal would be appalling if I were to return home after running away to join my lover. I can't go home. But I had to come. You understand, don't you, sir?"

"Surely your folks are more forgiving than that."

"I have my pride," she chafed. "I wouldn't disgrace them."

"Pride doesn't fill you when you're hungry," Fargo commented. "What if things don't work out with Dexeter?"

"I'll manage," she murmured.

"Do you have enough to get by?"

"For a few months. And I have Aphrodite and Plato. They're freed slaves, but they'd help me. And I have Jeffrey."

Fargo didn't offer his opinion of Jeffrey, but for Amelia's sake he hoped Dexeter was alive, on the mend, and hopelessly in love. "Amelia," Fargo murmured, pulling her closer, "it's not easy for a woman out here. If things don't work out, I think you should consider going home."

Amelia quivered against him. "On this journey, sir, you accused me of being a prude many times. I liked that," she admitted, running her fingers down his side until they rested on his pelvis. "I'm afraid my parents consider me something far worse." Her hand dropped down, seeking flesh that had

145

been ready and willing for too long. Fargo tensed and Amelia giggled.

"Maybe they were right," she confessed, half-laughing and half-crying.

"And maybe they just don't know the difference between good and bad," Fargo suggested.

"Oh, Mr. Fargo," Amelia whispered. "For a moment on that ice I actually hoped I would just keep sliding. I thought it would be easier that way. But you, sir, have reminded me of the pleasures in living. Remind me again," she breathed. "Please, Mr. Fargo, show me again."

"I don't know why I need to show you, honey." Fargo laughed as he slipped on top of her. "Seems to me you are one of those pleasures."

# 8

Fargo wasn't anxious to end his idyll with Amelia, but when four days passed and the Southerners hadn't shown up, he began to worry. The Southerners were traveling down the wide, relatively flat valley of the Blue. They should have been along within a day or two.

It was possible they hadn't liked Fargo's disappearing act and were merely looking for him. But as the days went by, Fargo felt the dread rising up and churning in his stomach. Fargo didn't like waiting, even if waiting with Amelia did have its compensations.

On the morning of the fifth day, Fargo was hidden in the trees just beyond the wagon road with nothing better to do than nap, when suddenly it sounded like a whole army coming down the valley. He heard them long before he could see them, mules and horses and more than one wagon, crawling along at not much more than an ambling walk.

Fargo didn't expect it to be the Southerners, but it was. Flanked by riders, Arbuthnot was sitting up on the lead wagon. After Fargo's raid on his camp, the senator must have decided to backtrack to Breckinridge to replace the whiskey, fetch more supplies, and recruit more allies. As the procession neared, Fargo recognized some of the members, and they weren't just southern kids out adventuring.

They were hardcases, every one. As the wagons drew closer, Long-Loop Lem came into view. A man who would do anything for a dollar, Lem looked to be the best of the lot. Fargo saw Cantwell Southey, who everyone in the territory knew was supposed to be in prison, and Manuel Chico, a half-breed Comanche who folks farther south often threatened their children with to get them to do their chores.

As the horses and wagons tossed up dust, Fargo felt the knot tightening in his belly. He crept through the trees, surveying the caravan. He saw three wagons: one open and piled with crates, one small cook wagon, and the familiar trade wagon. From concealment, Fargo scanned the faces of the riders and peered into the wagons. For a mile, he paralleled the Southerners, moving soundlessly through the woods as he studied, counted, and took stock. Then, he hurried back to the Ovaro and rode hell-bent for camp.

"Pack up," he shouted at Amelia. "We've got to move."

Amelia rushed up to him. "Is something wrong?" she demanded, the fear showing in her eyes.

"Yeah," Fargo muttered, but he didn't try to explain it to her.

As Fargo wrestled with the bedrolls and saddlebags, he figured he would explain what he knew about Arbuthnot, Smith, and Dexter on the road, but he doubted that what he had to say would comfort her any. Dexter was missing; he hadn't been with the Southerners this time.

Retracing Arbuthnot's route was easy, since Arbuthnot had been traveling with wagons and keeping to the road. But Fargo didn't see any sign of Dexter that day, and there was no use in overtiring the horses. They made camp.

On the way there, Fargo hadn't whitewashed Dexter's situation. He figured it was bad, and he had told Amelia as much. But although Amelia was subdued, she managed to do her part, building a fire and cooking their dinner, but her industry was a pale version of her normal energetic bustling. She clung to Fargo that night. And in the morning, her attempted smiles wrenched at his heart.

Fargo felt he was going in the wrong direction. Obviously, the Southerners were up to something big, and in all probability Dexter was dead.

Dexter couldn't have traveled with the Southerners so long without suspecting something, and Arbuthnot and Smith were pretty careless about men's lives. They had come after Fargo before he had posed a threat to them, so in all probability they had left behind a suspicious, consumptive painter.

The Southerners traveled slow, Fargo told himself. He could catch up. But that night he felt there was treachery in a woman's arms even when she wasn't particularly treacherous. Near dawn, Amelia woke. Her body was hot against his and they were both tangled in her hair.

"I owe you much, Mr. Fargo," she whispered, still ridiculously formal in her choice of address in spite of their position. "Soon we'll be going our separate ways, and there's little a woman can offer. But if you ever feel in need of food or shelter . . ." She let the suggestion dangle and gave instead what was of more immediate interest.

And Fargo had promised her he would find Dexter. Perhaps, it would be safe to spare three days or maybe four, but no more. After all, promises or no, Dexter was one man, and Arbuthnot was heading toward the Utes with an army.

Although Arbuthnot's promises and trade goods probably wouldn't have stirred the Utes, Indians could be persuaded to violence a might easier at gunpoint. Indians were warriors, born and bred in a warrior's culture. And violence was really all Arbuthnot wanted.

Once on the warpath? It was unlikely the whites would consider the provocation that sent the Indians out ravaging. After a while maybe the Indians would simmer down—maybe not. But if there were too many stories of atrocities, it was all too likely the whites would never let them.

In the afternoon, Fargo and Amelia came upon a side road that wound up into the foothills of the Gore Range. Dismounting, Fargo studied the narrow track. "You stay here," he ordered Amelia.

It wasn't much of a road, but the Southerners had been this way. Although it had probably been no more than an overnight stop, Fargo took no chances. The presence of a guard at the end of the road rewarded Fargo's vigilance, even if the man did appear to be doing more drinking than guarding.

His presence undetected, Fargo studied both the cabin and the filthy, grizzled guard. The man lolled by a tree a considerable distance from the cabin, with a jug perched on one knee and a pistol carelessly resting on his belly. He had a badly scarred face and a certain air that made him indisputably of the same ilk as the rest of Arbuthnot's new friends.

Then Fargo studied his own position. "Anybody home?" he called.

The guard started firing before bothering to greet his visitor. But Fargo was expecting it. Before the first bullet flew, Fargo had dropped and rolled. Bringing up the Sharps, he took careful aim and fired back.

"You should have been more careful with ammunition,"

Fargo muttered as the man's body slumped back against the tree. "No sense wasting it."

There was no noise from the cabin as Fargo waited tensely before he hazarded a stealthy trip to the side wall. Edging around to the door, he kicked it open. But nothing happened.

Inside, the cabin stank to high heaven, and Fargo approached the man on the cot, figuring he'd been dead for days. But the man's flesh was hot to the touch, and Fargo found himself staring down at Stephen Dexeter, thinking Dexeter would have been better off dead.

Amelia burst into the cabin behind Fargo, and he turned, trying to block Dexeter from her view.

"What are you doing here?" Fargo demanded.

"I heard gunfire."

"That's when you're supposed not to barge in," Fargo chided.

Amelia approached slowly, peering beyond Fargo at the man in the bed. "Is he dead?" she whispered. "Oh, God, it's Stephen," she cried. And before Fargo could stop her, she was on her knees beside the bed, weeping hysterically and calling Dexeter's name.

Dexeter was in sorry shape. The cabin was as filthy as the man outside who had tended it, and the unconscious Dexeter had been left to rot in his own excrement. Fargo grabbed Amelia around the waist and pulled her backward away from the bed. Turning her around, he tried to hold her, but she fought like a wild thing to get back to Dexeter's side.

So Fargo pushed her out the door. "Take a walk," Fargo ordered. "You won't be able to help him till you calm down."

Going back to the cot, Fargo didn't really believe there was any help for Dexeter. The Southerners had beaten him to within an inch of his life, but they had left him alive for some reason. It was the scum in the yard who had come closest to killing Dexeter. It was obvious Dexeter hadn't received even the rudiments of care.

Dexeter was gray, his lips were parched and cracked, and his skin was hot and dry to the touch. Fargo cursed the Southerners for not at least taking off the man's shirt before they laid on the whip. The garment was stiff with dried blood and there would no doubt be bits of cloth in the wounds.

Wielding his knife, Fargo cut away the shirt.

He had hoped it was too early in the season for flies, but the flesh underneath was alive and writhing with maggots. Fargo swallowed back the bile rising in his throat and went outside to fetch water, whiskey, and some of Amelia's fresh linen. And then he set to doing what had to be done.

Dexter was unconscious, but few men ever slip so far away that they can't feel excruciating pain, and Dexter was no exception. Just the manipulation taken to strip away soiled linen and clothing increased the man's agony. Angrily, Fargo tossed the filth aside to be burned later. Then he fought his nausea and went to work trying to ignore all but his task as Dexter moaned and twisted under his knife.

Fargo didn't see the difference, he heard it. Dexter was awake; he grasped the side of the cot in both hands and with enormous effort held back the sounds of his pain.

"You've got to stop them," he mumbled. "Arbuthnot, the others, they plan . . ." Dexter managed to turn, and the eyes that met Fargo's were filled with something more intense than the pain. "The Utes to the north, war, riders," Dexter breathed. He drew another ragged breath and grasped Fargo's arm with one hand. "They have gifts, tobacco, sugar. They plan attack. From the inside. At night. Utes. Then Cheyenne. Sioux, Arapaho, they plan . . ."

"I'll stop them," Fargo muttered. "Right now we've got to take care of you."

But it was one thing cutting on an unconscious man, another entirely torturing a conscious one.

While running the knife blade through the flame of a candle, Fargo saw how Dexter braced himself. The lash wounds were ulcerated and filled with pestilence. They needed to be deeply lanced to let them bleed freely. Fargo thought he'd give Dexter a few minutes to build his strength, and Dexter waited.

But then Dexter turned, and the gray eyes seemed less troubled. "Don't look so pained," he rasped, attempting a weak smile. "It's my flesh you scourge, not your own." He lay quiet and still, but with every muscle tensed as the knife carved at his wounds.

Impressed by the man's almost superhuman fortitude, Fargo pressed down on the inflamed flesh, forcing the pus to roil to the surface and wiping it aside until it oozed clearly. Then he washed Dexter's back, threw whiskey across it, and changed the linen once more, only to reheat the blade and begin again. The second time, Fargo slashed at the ravished flesh more deeply, letting the cleansing blood flow before he bound the wounds. Long before Fargo finished, Dexter had slipped back into a merciful unconsciousness.

Fargo had figured Dexter would be the aristocratic, artistic type, with gaunt cheeks, narrow lips, and a pinched nose, and there was some of that in Dexter's face. He was far too thin. But he certainly wasn't a simpering dandy. He had been through hell, and he was still breathing. And his features weren't bad, either. Fargo figured most folks would consider Dexter pretty handsome when he wasn't so gray—a fair match for Amelia.

"See what you can do about cleaning this place up," Fargo commanded Amelia as he stepped outside.

Fargo gulped down fresh air as he dug a grave for the dead guard. He had done what he could, and from here on, it was just waiting. But he didn't have time to wait. On the other hand, what was he supposed to do?

Leave Amelia with a man who would probably be a corpse within two days? Or trust the woman to leave her dead lover and find her way back to a town alone? Or perhaps he was just supposed to dig an extra hole in the yard and instruct her to bury Dexter when the time came. Although he felt the guard deserved to get dug up by coyotes, Fargo nevertheless covered the shallow grave with rocks before he went on a long walk, hoping to wear off the feeling that time was passing.

When Fargo returned after dark, the cabin was clean enough, but it reeked of rotgut whiskey. He wrinkled his nose in distaste.

"There wasn't enough soap," Amelia explained. "And then I remembered my mammie saying that most anything that would take the shine off a mirror would do for cleaning. The dead guard had an ample supply."

"What about him?" Fargo asked.

"He's been talking, rambling, but he's not lucid. I managed to get him to swallow a few spoonfuls of broth."

Her eyes were pleading for Fargo to reassure her, but he wasn't going to lie. He thought Dexter's chances were pretty poor.

Fargo slept outside that night. In the morning he found

Amelia, half-asleep but still sitting on a chair beside Dexeter's bed with an open book neglected on her lap.

"There's been no change," she murmured.

"You get some air and sleep. I'll watch for a while."

Fargo settled back with nothing better to do than pick up Amelia's book. But it was a silly story by a lady named Austen about a young girl in love with a sissified preacher who didn't seem to have any idea what a man was supposed to do with a woman. After reading a few chapters, Fargo figured he knew why Amelia had lugged the book so far without bothering to finish it. He felt his impatience festering as he tried to concentrate on pages that held no interest.

"You're Skye Fargo, aren't you?" Dexeter asked.

Fargo turned to stare at the man in the bed. "Yes," Fargo agreed. He hadn't really expected Dexeter to ever come to again. "There's some broth. You'd better take some before I check those wounds."

Dexeter struggled to sit up, the strain of the attempt clear in his tense features. "If you'd put that in a cup, I think I can manage," he said as he watched Fargo fetch the broth. "I never liked being spoon-fed, even by my mother." Dexeter clasped the cup determinedly, but his hands were unsteady and shaking. "You have to go," he told Fargo. "I'll manage here by myself."

"You won't have to," Fargo reasoned. "I'm not alone."

"The woman," Dexeter murmured. "I'd thought there was a woman here." He smiled, but the expression was so weary it was hard to credit.

"You're lucky to be alive."

"You call this luck?" Dexeter joked as he held out his cup to Fargo. Fargo took it, since Dexeter's hands were trembling too badly to hold it still. "It wasn't luck, it was money," Dexeter sighed as Fargo checked his wounds. "I have resources Arbuthnot feels I should sign over to him—before my last rites are conducted."

The lacerations were scabbed over, some of them a bit red and raw-looking, but it was nothing untoward. "Looks better than I thought it would," Fargo admitted.

"You wouldn't happen to know who it is that usually funds Arbuthnot, would you?" Fargo asked as he finished rewrapping bandages around Dexeter's torso.

"Certainly," Dexeter answered, leaning his head back on

the pillow and closing his eyes. "Fools," Dexeter murmured tiredly. "Men easily swindled by a dignified ex-senator with fine social connections. Men who buy false mining stock and empty promises. Men who trust a pretentious, fanatical popinjay to make them a fortune."

"They're not in on it?"

"No," Dexeter replied. "Feelings run high in the South, but there's still hope generated by the upcoming elections. Secessionists are a blind, embittered breed, but I don't think very many would advocate violence right now. I only hope it stays that way."

"Considering how fast you Southerners are with dueling pistols, I kind of doubt it will," Fargo commented as he put away the first-aid paraphernalia.

"What you must think of us," Dexeter meditated wearily. "I was once so proud of being a southern gentleman. We had a dream. Of an agrarian paradise. Of beauty. Of Greek temples and fair ladies and fine manners. Of wealth and civility and culture."

"I've been South," Fargo objected. "Seems to me most folks were black or poor white trash. It was a mighty exclusive dream."

"You're right, of course," Dexeter agreed readily. He opened his eyes and tried to sit up straighter, but the difficulty in the attempt showed in his taut expression. "You have to go now," Dexeter insisted. "Once I may have wrapped myself in silk and lace, but I'm stronger than you think. It's time you introduced me to your gentle companion. Though I fear she has probably seen much of me already, at my worst."

"You know something, Dexeter? You make me think there's hope for the South."

"A fine compliment." Dexeter laughed. "But I'm a Westerner now." Dexeter's laughter wound into a wheezy cough, but he suppressed it and Fargo began to think the man was going to make it.

Fargo found Amelia curled in her bedroll, with the canvas pulled up to block out the sun. "Amelia, he's awake," Fargo told her. "And waiting. I think he's going to get better."

Amelia glanced toward the cabin and turned absolutely white. "You will come with me?" she whispered.

"Sure," Fargo agreed, but he nearly had to push her through the door.

Amelia had come halfway across a continent to see her Dexeter, but now her courage seemed to have failed her altogether. She stood just inside the doorway looking as if she were ready to bolt, and Fargo hovered behind her, ready to catch her before she could get to the trees.

"Amy?" Stephen whispered. Forgetting his condition, Dexeter sat up and leaned forward, gasping as the sudden movement stretched the torn tissue in his back.

"Stephen," Amelia cried when she heard him gasp. Then she launched herself at him with the same energy that had nearly knocked Fargo off a mountain.

A fleeting spasm of pain crossed Dexeter's face as Amelia settled against his chest, but he recovered almost instantly. "Amy, what are you doing here?" he scolded. "This is no place for a woman. You should be home where it's safe."

"Oh, Stephen," she whimpered, "I've been so worried. Why did you just leave? Why didn't you tell me you were sick?"

Dexeter held Amelia, stroking her hair. "Amy, why did you come?" he whispered. "How am I ever going to give you up again?"

"You're not. Oh, please, Stephen, tell me you're not."

Fargo reckoned Amelia had won, since Dexeter wore the face of a man hopelessly in love. Fargo had to admit Amelia had a way of growing on you, but he was just as glad it wasn't him wearing that dazed expression.

"Dexeter," Fargo interrupted, "the guard's horse is out in back. When you're better, do you think the two of you can make it back to Denver?"

"We'll make it," Dexeter assured him.

"Good," Fargo muttered, turning to the door.

"Wait," Dexeter protested. "I want to thank you for everything. And for Amy. Fargo, be careful."

"I always am," Fargo mumbled as Amelia turned to stare at him. "I've got to go," he maintained, and then, not believing in long good-byes, he left. He was saddling his horse when Amelia ran out.

"Stephen sent me," she said, "to say good-bye."

"That's nice," Fargo admitted.

"Stephen knows," she murmured.

"You told him?"

"I didn't have to. He's very intuitive. Mr. Fargo, I love Stephen. I wouldn't want you to think, because of what happened with you, that I'd be a bad wife."

"I never thought that," Fargo protested. "I'm not in the market for a wife, but if I were . . ." Fargo smiled as he shrugged.

"And if you were, sir, I might have accepted your generous proposal," she teased. "But I've had the most worrisome feeling you don't like the way I furnish your camp." Abruptly, Amelia hurtled toward Fargo, nearly toppling him with her embrace. "I love Stephen Dexeter," she whispered against his chest, "but I love you too, Skye Fargo. Take care of yourself." With that, Amelia whirled around and ran back into the cabin. And Fargo headed north.

The wagon road, slushy from the spring melt, still showed deep churned ruts from Arbuthnot's and Smith's load of trade goods. The Trailsman rode parallel to the road, staying up in the rolling foothills where the grass and sagebrush met the forest. The footing was firmer, and if anybody started shooting at him, he was right next to some cover.

At the edge of an aspen grove overlooking the lush bottomland, the Ovaro got skittish. Noticing that the cawing of crows had suddenly overwhelmed the usual bird chatter, Fargo dismounted with pistol in hand and crept up warily toward where the Ovaro didn't want to go.

The man who had troubled the Ovaro while causing such chatter among the crows would never bother anybody again. He lay there on his belly, sprawled among the greening aspen, with an arrow shaft protruding from his back. Circling the corpse, Fargo saw a bloody ring of mush where the man's hair had been. The body's outlines looked familiar, and when Fargo pushed it over with his boot, he recognized Long-Loop Lem staring up at him.

All the signs looked Indian, and Fargo quickly picked up tracks from two unshod ponies leading to and from the site. Going away, one's tracks didn't sink in as deeply. Finding Lem's killer might mean some answers, so Fargo consoled the Ovaro about how awful fresh blood smelled to horses, and followed the tracks.

Just where an old cottonwood limb shaded the trail, both sets of pony tracks got shallow, and Fargo knew that if he swung around to the other side of the trees, he'd find some moccasin prints there, or else where someone had tried to cover up the presence of such prints. Fargo scanned the countryside and his memory for the likeliest bushwhacking spot and dismounted, sending the Ovaro on down the trail for a rest at the river while he toted the Sharps up a patch of boulders.

It was one mighty surprised Ute who felt Fargo's Sharps prodding his back a few minutes later. Short and squat, the buckskin-clad brave rose slowly and turned, Lem's fresh scalp dangling from his belt. Something like an admiring smile crossed the Ute's round face when his brown eyes met Fargo's icy blue stare.

"Hay-yo. This was his day to die. Not yours. Not mine."

Not surprised by the language, because many Utes spoke English, Fargo took in the brave's perch. Other than the man's belt knife, there wasn't a weapon in sight—no rifle, no pistol, not even the bow and arrow. The brave had been up here just to watch, not to ambush. Fargo lowered the Sharps and introduced himself.

"I am called Tabernash," the Ute replied. "And I have been told much about you by the white men who visit my people at the stinking springs."

"I'll bet you have," Fargo nodded, allowing himself to smile.

"Any man who is their enemy is a good person." Tabernash broke into a broad grin and held up the scalp. "This man tried to rape one of my women, a good worker I stole myself from the Arapaho. This morning he rode off on my favorite horse I took from the Comanche. I followed him. His death song was long. He whined like a puppy. Then I decided to wait for you."

"They told you I was on my way?" Fargo asked.

Tabernash nodded. "They have sentries. They plan to kill you when you come in sight of the springs."

Arbuthnot and Smith had arrived early yesterday, distributing flour, sugar, tobacco, gunpowder, and whiskey, all of which the Utes were happy enough to take. They'd parlayed with Chief Sowawick and got about as far as they had with Chief Niwot over on the other side of the mountains. But more and more hardcase whites were showing up at the hot springs every day.

The way Tabernash talked, the white men were as randy as billy goats, tossing women down right in the open. And his own brothers were racing their ponies through camp and burning down tepees when they weren't writhing in agony. It sounded like this last load of firewater Arbuthnot had gotten was even worse than the one Fargo had confiscated.

"You do want those white men to leave, don't you?" Fargo asked Tabernash as they started working their way down the steep forested hillside to the horses standing next to the river, a thousand feet below. Taking the Ute's grunt for a "yes," Fargo mentioned Coyote the Trickster, a prominent character in Ute fireside tales.

Tabernash paused for a short prayer or whatever. It must have been effective, because by the time they got to the river, found the horses, and cached Lem's scalp and other goods, they had a plan that the old trickster would have appreciated.

The sun had barely cleared the Front Range the next morning when Tabernash rode home. In his medicine bag was a twenty-dollar gold piece that he and Fargo had hammered with rocks. Gold was so malleable that it took only a few minutes to make a coin look a lot like a big nugget fresh out of the gravel. They cut up another double eagle and beat on the pieces to make it look as though Tabernash had stumbled across the richest gravel since California.

Fargo waited on the ridge, looking down on an Indian village so overstocked with white men it looked like a saloon on a Saturday night.

Only twice did Tabernash need to recount how he'd been out hunting elk in some meadows north and west of the hot springs. He'd bent low to quench his thirst in the creek. Right under his big hooked nose he'd seen these shiny yellow rocks that white men liked so much.

Tabernash, being an ignorant redskin who didn't know the value of gold, didn't feel like going back up there soon. Gesticulating madly, he warned the white men the valley was worthless because it held no elk. But he was glad enough to draw a map in the dirt for the excited men who clustered around him and eyed the huge nuggets.

The first time Tabernash told his story and showed off the nuggets, he had an audience of only four hard cases. The second time, there were nine. After that, he'd lost all potential of any more audience, because all the white riffraff were on their way to the great gold discovery. Following Tabernash's map would take them into some deadfall-filled box canyons that they wouldn't get out of in much less than a week, if they didn't freeze to death first.

Arbuthnot and Smith shouldn't have acted as surprised as they did, Fargo thought from his hillside vantage above the steaming hot springs, since their followers were men who would do most anything for easy money. But Arbuthnot and Smith didn't seem to be considering that as they stood before their tent, shaking their fists and cussing a lot as the last of their gang rode away.

Ezekiel Smith pulled out a pistol and fired wildly, hitting a hapless mule rather than one of the men. But Smith provided a clear shot for Fargo, who exhaled softly and squeezed the trigger of his Sharps. The mountainsides echoed with its blast. Smith remained standing for a moment, then fell in a heap, the tails of his frock coat fluttering as the man collapsed softly into the dirt.

Sometimes men just stood there, shocked, when someone nearby went down that way, and if Julius Arbuthnot had done that, Fargo would have had time to reload the Sharps and end the man's career of inciting warfare between North and South and between white men and red men. But Arbuthnot took off like a turpentined dog as soon as Smith started to fall.

By the time Fargo's single-shot Sharps was reloaded, the onetime senator had run into the midst of the Ute camp, moving with considerable speed for a man of his girth. While Fargo watched through his sights, hoping for a clear shot, Arbuthnot sped past two or three astonished men and reached the last tepee, where a slight girl, no more than eight or nine years old, sat by the entrance, grinding corn. She looked up just in time to see Arbuthnot's beefy arm crook itself around her neck and drag her toward the flimsy rope corral where the horses were penned.

Arbuthnot turned, holding the girl before him as half a dozen braves approached. He pulled up his dragoon pistol and held it against the frozen girl's right ear. Fargo couldn't hear what Arbuthnot was saying, but it didn't matter. He had the message as soon as he saw the Ute men step back while Arbuthnot and the girl disappeared into the horses. Knowing they would emerge mounted on the other side after cutting the barrier and scattering the horses, Fargo whistled for the Ovaro.

They pounded down the hillside to the flats along the Grand River amid Ute men trying to catch their horses. Fargo had barely cleared the confusion when he heard hoofbeats in the streamside gravel and turned to see Tabernash, getting the ride of his life on one of the husky wagon mules. Truth be told, the short Ute looked ridiculous, his stumpy legs forced almost straight out by the width of the mule's back, holding on to the close-cropped mane while the gray-haired critter kicked and sunfished, trying to get rid of its unaccustomed burden.

"Hay-yo, Fargo," Tabernash shouted. "That is my child he took."

The Ute's face was grim as he caught up to Fargo, locking his knees up on the mule's neck so he could kick the beast's nose every time the brute got contrary notions. Tabernash mentioned several notions for Arbuthnot's departure.

As nearly as Fargo could figure from the garbled talk of a worried father, Tabernash wanted to cut off Arbuthnot's balls and ram them down his throat, then string a pole between trees and hang Arbuthnot there, feet up and head down, with his scalped head suspended about a foot above a small fire. Arbuthnot could twist and wiggle for a while, trying to keep his brains from being fried, and then Tabernash planned to skin the still-living senator and stake him to an anthill.

"No," Fargo finally interjected. "This one's mine."

"He took my daughter."

Arguing with Tabernash would only waste time and energy, Fargo could tell, so they silently followed the pony tracks for another mile or so. Just as Fargo had figured, Arbuthnot wouldn't keep a hostage for any longer than necessary. So it wasn't exactly unexpected when they came up on the slender, doeskin-clad girl, lying still as death in the greening willows, blood in her braided black hair.

Dismounting, Fargo bent low over the tiny form, then grabbed a fistful of pointed willow leaves and held them under her nose. The leaves quivered. He looked up to Tabernash with a nod and a smile. From the looks of things, Arbuthnot had pushed her off the horse, and the girl had hit the ground headfirst while he rode on. She'd have a nasty bump and a mean headache when she came around, but Fargo felt certain she would come around—her breath and pulse were regular.

While Tabernash cradled his daughter in his arms and

muttered softly to her, the mule took off for parts unknown. That was probably for the best. The slip of a girl had already been dropped hard once today, and the odds were against her and her father staying on the mule all the way if they tried to ride back to camp.

Tabernash lifted his round brown eyes to Fargo. "You will kill him?" The Trailsman nodded. Tabernash started to rise with his child, but Fargo motioned him down.

"This isn't the time to have dead white men around your camp," Fargo explained. "Make sure you bury Smith, the man I shot, and bury Lem, the man you killed. Bury them in a secret place so deep that no man or animal will find them." Tabernash looked puzzled, so Fargo continued. "The Blue Sleeves will come if you do not hide those bodies."

Tabernash nodded and rose, slinging his knocked-out daughter over his shoulder like a sack of flour. "You are a good person, Fargo." With his free hand, Tabernash reached into his medicine bag and pulled out the nuggets they had fabricated. "Do not forget your shining rocks."

Fargo waved them back and the bow-legged Ute smiled, then turned toward camp, ambling along like a bear. Already they could hear horses approaching from that direction.

Following the hard-struck tracks of the galloping pony tracks eastward, up the broad valley of Middle Park, Fargo wondered how long the portly Arbuthnot could maintain that pace. He had to be pushing mighty hard. But he'd just find himself jammed against the Continental Divide, that great wall of rock and snow, so Fargo kept the Ovaro to a trot as they topped a gentle rise in the fresh grass that carpeted the valley.

Near the bottom of the swell, a paint pony was still catching its breath next to a placid burro. Fargo's pinto got annoyed by the smell, and he had to prod the Ovaro forward.

Fargo didn't have to dismount to see what had happened. A well-outfitted prospector had happened along the Grand River, and had the misfortune to encounter Arbuthnot. They'd stopped to chat, and instead of exchanging gossip, Arbuthnot had fired his dragoon pistol into the back of the prospector's head. The soft lead bullet, expanding as it encountered bone and flesh, had taken most of the man's face with it when it came out the front.

So Arbuthnot now rode a fresh horse. Even worse, Fargo

thought, was that this prospector had to have come in over the Divide, which now loomed to the east. The spring melt-off had progressed so much that some sort of crossing was possible along this towering stretch of mountains. Fargo couldn't count on backing Arbuthnot against that massive gray wall. The killer could just keep going east, over the mountains and down to Denver City, and only the devil knew where Arbuthnot might head after that.

The tracks would lead to the crossing, but Fargo needed to get there before Arbuthnot did. Where would it be? Everything had changed since the gold rush, with men pushing roads and trails into the most remote and forbidding country.

Fargo recalled that on the bleak shoulder of James Peak, which dominated the skyline and looked almost close enough to grab, there was one ridge known as the Hogback. Constant winds scoured the snow off its barren shattered granite. The east approach, up the narrow canyon of South Boulder Creek, was steep and miserable, but the west side eased down into Middle Park. That had to be where the prospector had crossed and where Arbuthnot was headed.

Hoping the Utes had enough sense to bury the prospector when they came across the corpse, Fargo pushed straight into the mountains before him instead of following Arbuthnot's tracks south. Just where Arbuthnot would head into the mountains, there was an alpine bog that could swallow whole wagon trains, and the killer ought to lost at least two hours struggling across and around it. Once the senator got above the morass and began climbing Boulder Pass in earnest, Fargo would be waiting in the trees.

But for one stretch of ice, it would have worked that way after Fargo and the Ovaro pushed along game trails in the timber for several hours, reaching the path that led up to the Hogback. On a recent warm day, the snowmelt had come down the hill in a big sheet, spreading across this open spot. Then the water had been frozen in place for a few days until the spring runoff got more serious.

The big pinto lost its footing on the slick stuff just as Fargo was preparing to dismount and lead it past the treacherous zone. The Trailsman was pitched sideways, his body sliding down until his shoulder hit a boulder with bruising force and jammed him into the rocks while his Colt bounced on down the mountain. Every way he twisted sent burning spasms of pain down his arm and along his spine, and by the time Fargo worked his way back out, Arbuthnot was standing a few yards downhill, displaying a satisfied smile and dragoon pistol.

"So we finally meet, Mr. Fargo." Arbuthnot's bushy eyebrows lifted as he drawled. "Excuse me. We haven't been formally introduced. I am Senator Julius Arbuthnot of the sovereign state of South Carolina."

"So I've heard," Fargo muttered. No telling where the pistol was, and the way his arm hurt, he couldn't even reach the throwing knife in his boot, let alone make it fly toward Arbuthnot's throat. The glare from Fargo's blue eyes matched the senator's in intensity as Arbuthnot continued.

"This great nation was founded upon twin pillars of principle," the senator announced. "Property rights and states' rights. And there are scoundrels, nay, even blackguards, who conspire to deprive us of those rights. We shall fight for them, Mr. Fargo, we shall protect our constitutional rights. If it comes to war, then there shall be war, especially if that baboon Lincoln is elected by the abolitionist betrayers of our sacred covenant and constitution."

It's bad enough, Fargo thought as Arbuthnot went on, that the man planned to kill him. But did this blustering windbag have to make Fargo suffer through a political speech first? Fargo sat up straighter on the ice, wondering if his butt would freeze totally before Arbuthnot got around to shooting him.

Arbuthnot orated for a few more minutes, the dragoon pistol steady on Fargo's forehead, before pausing to catch his breath. "It is a noble cause, Mr. Fargo. We are fighting for our traditional livelihood, to protect and preserve an institution sanctioned by God." Arbuthnot's voice shifted up a register after the man paused to gulp in some of the thin, cold air. "You may die here unmourned, Mr. Fargo. Or you might save yourself by joining our cause."

Fargo made himself look interested as he rearranged his position so that some new chunk of his backside could grow icicles. "You'd want me?" he asked Arbuthnot.

"You would be amply paid for your considerable skills," Arbuthnot replied. "Certainly you can see that our cause might well be your cause."

As he rested his left hand on an unstable rock that poked above the ice, Fargo tried to count up just how many recent murders could be blamed on this oily self-serving hypocrite.

Worrying the rock by wiggling it like a loose tooth, Fargo kept his eyes on Arbuthnot. "I can't say as I hold with starting wars, Senator."

"Can't you see that I am trying to prevent a greater war?" Arbuthnot replied. "If enough federal troops are brought out here to quell the Indian uprisings, then the South might be able to leave the Union without general bloodshed. Otherwise, a bloody war may engulf us all, whether we wish for one or not. All that South Carolina desires is to be left in peace, to prosper as an inviolate institution."

The speech might have continued for hours, but for being interrupted when the senator's feet went out from under him after Fargo got the rock loose and sent it sliding toward Arbuthnot's tooled-leather boots. Fargo coasted down the ice right along after it, stopping when he piled into Arbuthnot and rolled atop the portly senator.

The man had kept hold of the pistol, and he was trying to bring it around on Fargo, whose left hand gripped the senator's wrist like a vise, squeezing with crushing force until the stubby fingers released the weapon. But when Fargo reached for it, the senator's fingers had found the barrel. He brought it up like a club and smashed it into Fargo's temple with enough power to roll the Trailsman off him.

It was foolish to be in a hurry getting up on this ice, as Arbuthnot quickly discovered. Dazed and barely able to see through the mist of blood covering his eyes, Fargo felt Arbuthnot's bulk land on his legs, and kicked furiously while wiping his face with a sleeve, trying to clear his vision. The weight slid off and Fargo sat up to see Arbuthnot coming at him on all fours with the look of a she-bear worried about her cubs. The Trailsman pulled his long, muscular legs back against his chest for protection.

Arbuthnot's clumsy lunge put him atop Fargo. No matter how much Fargo tried to straighten his legs, Arbuthnot's hand would not leave the Trailsman's throat, and Fargo's only good arm was pinned behind him, getting ground into the ice as they wrestled. Gasping to no effect and gritting through the pain, Fargo pushed his throbbing right arm down between them toward his boot. Twice his grasp slipped before he could pull out the knife, and all that time Arbuthnot was intent on crushing his windpipe.

At least his eyes were clear of blood now, so the Trailsman

could see the astonished expression on Arbuthnot's enraged face as the blade entered near his belly button and sliced toward his breastbone. Arbuthnot's grip on Fargo's throat weakened and Fargo sucked in air, working the knife with all the strength he could will into his battered arm and cramped hand.

Julius Arbuthnot rolled back, catching his bloody intestines in his hands. Fargo wearily slid himself to the edge of the ice patch and used a sapling to pull himself up.

Arbuthnot was still alive, blood spurting out of the gash that had been his belly. The pain and realization hit the man at the same time. He started to scream, a horrified shrill wail that stopped only for labored breaths.

He might last a day or so like that, Fargo thought, unless a coyote came along sooner and started nibbling at his unprotected guts. And the son of a bitch deserved every moment of such agony. But Fargo had seen and heard enough. Arbuthnot's unfired pistol lay only a step or two away. Fargo stumbled over, picked it up, and emptied the gun into the senator's head.

Under the May sunshine and a brilliant blue sky, Denver City looked better than anything Fargo had seen for the past week, as he rode into town anxious for a hot bath, a decent meal, and the chance to relax with some whiskey. When Fargo had last passed through, the livery stable had sat on the edge of town, but now fresh buildings of rough-cut lumber extended past it for three blocks, with more under construction.

Stopping in the stable yard, Fargo didn't even have time to dismount before he saw a white-haired, grizzled black man put down some harness and stride toward him.

"Hello, Mr. Fargo," Plato called out. "Want me to take care of that fine horse?"

Fargo swung out of the saddle. "Why, certainly, Mr. Plato," he said. At hearing the "Mr." before his own name, the black man straightened and nodded. "If you be lookin' for Mr. MacFadden, he be inside."

Fargo thanked Plato and handed him a quarter before stepping across to the office, where MacFadden insisted that this was as good a time as any to stroll down to Uncle Dick Wooten's saloon, where three galvanized tubs had just been installed upstairs, so that a man could wash the trail dust off the inside and outside of his body at the same time, if he wanted to.

"The talk against the Indians has simmered down plenty," MacFadden explained as they worked their way up the crowded street. Some of the more enterprising merchants had installed boardwalks in front of their shops, but they couldn't seem to agree on just how high the walks should sit, so there were toe-stubbing risers and jarring surprise drops to disturb their easy pace.

"You got here about two days too late for the big wedding," MacFadden continued. "That Dexeter fellow barely had strength to stand up, but he and Amelia got hitched up all good and proper. Then they went right on back into the mountains. Dexeter plans on painting. And the lady boasted she knew all there was to know about living in the wilderness, 'cause you taught her. Knowing you, her know-how will probably suit for a honeymoon."

They turned the corner, and Fargo saw a storefront with a long line of jostling men outside. He was about to ask if it was a new cathouse offering free samples, but then he noticed the horribly misspelled sign: ROKKY MOWNTEN LONDRY. MacFadden saw him looking that way and explained. "That little laundry belongs to Aphrodite—you remember, Amelia's servant?—and the talk is she's making more money by washin' clothes than any of us menfolk has made yet by washin' gold. Her first week, she cleared better'n thirty dollars."

"How'd that come about?" Fargo finally caught sight of Dick Wooten's saloon, one of the only genuine two-story buildings in Denver City.

"Oh, with Amelia up in the mountains having you protect her honor and whatever, little Jeffrey managed to lose their stake by spending about an hour at Tildondo's Gambling Emporium. So Aphrodite and Plato had to do something. We were glad enough to put Plato on at the stable, busy as things have been. Besides, Jeffrey didn't want to take the two of them along when he left."

Fargo nodded pleasantly and then began to wonder out loud. "Jeffrey left? I'd planned on you keeping that gallant shit-for-brains cavalier close to town."

"Well, likely it was Clara's idea for the two of them to head up to Montana Territory together. I reckon I'll miss

Clara," MacFadden said, "but I can't say I'm real sorry that he's gone."

The smell of whiskey, beer, soap, and hot water meant they were almost upon Wooten's saloon and bathhouse, where Fargo meant to soak until at least the first three layers of crud turned soft enough to scrape off his skin. Just before they got to the batwing doors, though, they were accosted.

Glowing red hair cascaded out from under her lace-trimmed bonnet, spilling onto creamy shoulders that her low-cut gown barely covered. Fargo first saw the twirling parasol, then the inviting big green eyes before his own eyes moved on down to ample cleavage that promised all manner of delight. After enjoying the sight for a moment or two, he raised his gaze to meet hers.

"Would you-all know where Ah can fahnd Mistah Skye Fahgo? Ah'm Miss Priscilla Peyton from Mobile, Alabama, an' Ah simply must get ovah the mountains to Salt Lake City. Ah've been told he's the best, an' Ah'm prepared to pay most handsomely for a guide." She stopped drawling to bat those long lashes while her dimples appeared, flanking a practiced smile.

For once, MacFadden was speechless.

"I can't say where you might find this Fargo character, ma'am," the Trailsman replied, "but this man here can certainly get you to Salt Lake. I'm proud to introduce you to Tom Mac-Fadden, one of the great up-and-coming scouts of the West."

With that, Fargo pushed the stable hand toward her and slipped inside the saloon, paying the bartender an extra four bits to bolt the door behind him after he went upstairs and settled into a steaming tub, bottle in hand.

*1861, northern Colorado, the Arapaho land
at the foot of Shadow Mountain where
the real shadow was the shadow of death . . .*


He didn't want company.

He didn't expect company.

He sure didn't welcome company.

He'd chosen the little hollow because it was sweet and warm and out of the way and smelled of cedar. He'd tied the horses just outside at the edge of the woods and he watched Molly Ludlum slip her blouse and skirt off and lay naked in front of him. She was as lovely as he remembered, all of a piece, a smallish girl but everything balanced, breasts, hips, legs. His lake-blue eyes moved appreciatively over her as he slid his own shirt off, undid his gun belt and dropped it on the star moss.

Molly reached arms up to him and her sweet breasts lifted, small brown-pink tips already growing firm. "Fargo," she breathed, "I didn't know how much I've missed you." He smiled as he sank down atop her and felt the soft-warm sensation of flesh against flesh, a sweet, sensuous touch that flooded his body with its unspoken message. He pulled Levi buttons open as he pressed his lips over one modest, beautifully cupped breast. He had just circled the tiny tip with his tongue when he heard the sudden, sharp sound of hoofbeats.

He drew his lips from the sweet mound and frowned as he let his ears become his eyes. One horse, he grunted silently, moving hard and fast just outside the wooded terrain. He stayed atop Molly as he listened, waited for the hoofbeats to pass but the frown dug deeper into his brow as he heard them veer and head straight for the hollow. His hand snapped out, yanked the big Colt from the holster on the moss beside him and half-turned as he heard the horse crash into the woods. He had the revolver raised as the horse burst into the little hollow and the rider reined to a skidding halt. Fargo's quick glance took in honey-wheat blond hair hanging down to the shoulders, gray-blue eyes in a finely featured face.

The girl stared at him half over Molly's naked form, shocked surprise in her eyes. "Oh, my," she bit out. Fargo lowered the Colt as he saw the surprise turn into disapproving disdain. "Sorry for the interruption," she said icily. "I saw your horses."

"The sight of horses always send you crashing hell-bent into the woods, honey?" Fargo asked with irritation and Molly pulled her blouse half over herself.

"I was looking for help. There are two wagons under Indian attack," she answered.

"Where?" Fargo asked.

"Half-mile or so west of here," the girl said. "I was on high land when I saw the attack. I turned and raced away to get help."

"How many Indians?" Fargo questioned.

"Maybe thirty? I didn't stay to count," she said tartly. "Well?"

"Well, what?" Fargo grunted.

"Don't just lay there and ask questions. Get your horse. We've got to help those wagons."

"Forget it," Fargo said and sat up. "It's all over by now."

"Maybe not. Maybe they're still holding out," the girl countered.

"Not likely," Fargo said grimly. He turned as he felt Molly's hand slide across his arm.

"You can't be sure," Molly said and he frowned at her.

"Sure enough. Besides, you two going to take on maybe thirty braves with me?" he speared.

Molly's lips tightened and she lowered her eyes, but he heard the girl's voice snap out words. "You could do something but it's plain you'd rather indulge in your own pleasures than try to help two wagons full of people," she said, contempt wrapped around each word.

"We saw a platoon of troopers riding patrol, not more than ten minutes ago," Fargo told her. "They were making a wide circle. Ride due north and you'll meet up with them. They're the kind of help you need."

The girl threw him a glare of gray-blue contempt. "Thank you for nothing. Do enjoy yourself," she flung at him scathingly and whirled her horse in a tight circle and charged out of the hollow. Fargo listened to the horse race out of the trees and onto open ground and felt Molly's eyes on him.

"You can't just let her ride off alone," Molly said, reproof in her voice. "Not with a war party on the rampage this near." He fixed her with a grim glare. "You know that's not right, Fargo," she said.

"Shit," Fargo muttered as he swung onto his side, yanked the gunbelt to him and rose to his feet. She was right, of course, he knew, and turned his back on her lovely nakedness as he strapped the gunbelt on. He swung around and pulled his shirt on and saw Molly had drawn her blouse over her dark, curly triangle. "You wait right here till I get back, you hear me?" he ordered. "Don't you get any fool notions about riding back to town alone."

"I'll stay right here, promise," Molly said. He tossed a grim grunt at her and strode from the little hollow to where he'd left the horses. With a smooth, swift motion, he swung onto the magnificent Ovaro and sent the horse into a full gallop. He picked up the girl's tracks at once, saw that she'd followed instructions and raced her horse northward, the line of hoof marks cutting clean and deep into the ground. He sent the Ovaro racing alongside the hoofprints and silently flung an oath into the wind.

The girl's intrusion seemed but one more surprise in a week of surprises. He'd ridden into Owlshead after bringing a cattle drive up from the Oklahoma territory and was surprised to find a military compound at one end of the town. No major line fort such as Kearny or Laramie but it did boast a blockhouse and a stockade. The second surprise was finding Molly Ludlum in Owlshead. It had been two years since he's last

seen her in Kansas in a town called Cragsville. She'd worked
for the local dance hall then, though she'd never been a fancy
girl. But she'd always been a hellion, not bothered by how
many eyebrows she raised, and he remembered all the pleasure times they'd had together. But small towns with preten-
sions could be cruel and he heard Molly had up and left one
day, with a flare and a flounce, he was sure. In any case, she
was gone when he'd stopped at Cragsville again and he'd
never learned what had become of her.

Not until seven days ago when he'd ridden into Owlshead.
Fargo smiled as he thought of how Molly had been as surprised and delighted as he. She'd flown into his arms in
the middle of Main Street but quickly pulled away. "It's all
different here, Skye," she had told him later. "I've a good
job caring for Ed Kroger's two kids and I teach Sunday
school every week."

"Sounds like you've changed into a right respectable young
woman, Molly," he had commented. "You telling me you
don't want to turn the clock back?"

Her smile had the sly mischievousness in it he used to
know so well. "I'm not all that respectable I can't remember," she said. "I just have to be careful now. No more
sticking my tongue out at the world."

"I'll find the place, you find the time," he'd said and her
eyes had carried anticipation in their brown orbs. But though
he'd found the little hollow, it had taken her a week to find
the moment and now it had all exploded. Appropriately unex-
pectedly, Fargo grunted as his thoughts snapped off when he
caught sight of honey-wheat hair. The girl was still riding
hard along a ribbon of open land bordered by shadbush on
one side and box elder on the other. But out of the corner of
his eye he caught the movement in the shadbush and slowed
the Ovaro immediately. He squinted into the distant trees and
picked out the two horses moving swiftly after the girl,
caught the flash of bronzed, naked torsos on agile Indian
ponies.

He turned and sent the Ovaro into the box elder on the
other side and put the horse into a gallop again. The girl was
completely unaware of the two riders in the shadbush, he
saw, as she bent forward in the saddle, her eyes searching

open land ahead for signs of the cavalry troop. The line of shadbush came to a sudden end another hundred yards on and Fargo had pulled almost abreast of the two riders when they burst into the open and pushed their ponies into a full-out gallop. He stayed in box elder and saw the girl turn in the saddle, suddenly aware of her pursuers as they moved out on each side of her. She tried to coax more speed from her horse but the light-brown mare was too tired to give any more. The two bronzed forms closed quickly on the girl and Fargo drew the Colt from its holster, grimaced and dropped the gun back in place. Maybe there were others nearby. A shot would surely bring them on the run and he didn't want that.

He swore under his breath, took the Ovaro out of the box elder as the two Indians converged on the girl. He saw her try to swerve, strike out with her left arm as they came alongside her. But one reached from his horse, wrapped both arms around her waist and pulled her from the saddle. He slowed his pony with his knees and half-fell, half-leaped to the ground with the girl still in his grip. The other Indian pulled to a halt, leaped to the ground and grabbed the girl by the legs as she tried to kick herself free. Fargo's hand reached down to the narrow holster around his calf and he drew the double-edged throwing knife known in some places as an Arkansas toothpick. The first Indian had pinned the girl's arms behind her while the other began to pull down her skirt and Fargo caught a glimpse of long, smooth legs. They were both absorbed in their quarry and he was within a dozen yards of them when they became aware of him. The one pulling the girl's skirt whirled, straightened and yanked a tomahawk from the waist of his breechclout.

Fargo charged straight at him as he bent low in the saddle and threw the perfectly balanced blade underhanded. It whistled through the air and took a half-second before the Indian saw it. He spun, tried to dive to his right but the knife slammed into his side and buried itself to the hilt between his upper ribs. The man fell forward to his knees, the tomahawk dropping from his hand and Fargo spurred the Ovaro straight at him. The Indian tried to get up and Fargo heard the horse's foreknee slam into his head as the Ovaro hurtled into and over him. Fargo reined up, leaped from the saddle and saw the Indian on his back, his head a bloodied, smashed object and his side a stream of red.

The other brave threw the girl aside as he leaped to his feet and drew a jagged-edged elkbone knife from his waistband. He began to circle and Fargo saw the girl push to her feet, stare with fear in her gray-blue eyes. "Get your horse," Fargo said to her as he began to circle with the Indian. "Get out of here and find those soldier boys." He flicked a glance at her and saw her hesitate. *"Now!"* he spit out and she backed a pace, turned and ran toward the light-brown mare. His eyes were back on the brave and he saw the Indian decide not to try to stop her. The man had long arms and a thin body. He'd be quick of hand and foot, Fargo knew, and he drew the Colt from its holster, turned the gun in his hand to grip the barrel.

The Indian came forward as he circled, feinted with the bone knife, but Fargo refused to bite. He feinted again and once more Fargo didn't react. The next would not be a feint, Fargo knew, and he set himself as the Indian came in again. The red man's arm came up, made a half-feint and then hurtled forward with the bone knife in a flat, slashing blow. Fargo drew his stomach in as he leaped backwards with both feet and knife grazed the front of his shirt. He brought the butt of the gun up in a short arc but the Indian's quickness pulled him away and the blow missed. Fargo ducked away to avoid a second follow-through, but the Indian was careful as well as quick and set himself again before moving forward.

The flash of wheat-honey hair racing away caught Fargo's eye as he circled with the Indian and this time he tried a feint. The brave ducked away and Fargo swung the butt of the gun again and once more the Indian pulled away. But this time the brave swung his body in a low half-crouch, came forward with quick, alternating steps, both hands moving spasmodically. Fargo gave ground and the brave followed until, with a lightning-quick motion, the Indian threw a chopping left fist and, as Fargo ducked away from the blow, lunged with the bone knife. Fargo let himself go down on his knees as the weapon grazed his temple and he silently cursed the man's surefooted quickness. He managed to bring his own left up in a short arc, all the strength of his shoulder muscles behind the blow, and sank his fist into the Indian's belly. The man grunted in pain as he staggered back and, with a few inches more room, Fargo brought the gun butt around in an upward arc.

The brave twisted away but the blow caught him a glancing blow alongside the cheek and he fell to one side. Fargo charged after him, the Colt raised to smash it down on his foe's head. But he'd been too eager and it was too late when he saw the kick flung backwards at him. The blow caught him in the stomach and he went backwards in pain, felt his feet go out from under him. He saw the long-armed body charging, the bone knife thrust out as if it were a lance. On his back, he half-rolled and the knife buried itself into the ground a fraction of an inch from his ear. He tried to roll again and felt one long, sinewy arm wrap itself around his neck. "Goddamn," Fargo swore as he used his powerful shoulders to push himself to his knees. The brave clung to him, kept one arm tight around his neck, a grip that would have forced most men back choking for breath. But he was too light to hold Fargo's powerful body and the big man rose, the Indian still clinging to him almost as a child clings piggyback to its father.

Fargo bent forward, swung his body in a tight circle and sent the brave sailing from him. He whirled as the Indian hit the ground, charged the thin form and saw the Indian scramble to his feet and managed to avoid the first sweeping blow of the heavy Colt. The Indian continued to scramble to get away and, in frustration and fury, Fargo brought the butt of the gun down with all his strength on the Indian's calf. The man gave a gasp of pain as his leg collapsed under him and he fell forward, tried to scramble again but his numbed calf refused to respond. He whirled, tried a kick with his other leg and Fargo took the blow against the side of his thigh as he brought the Colt down in a whistling arc. The heavy gun butt smashed into the Indian's temple and Fargo heard the sound of bone splintering. He drew back as the Indian twitched, long arms flailing against his sides spasmodically and then he lay still.

Fargo pushed himself to his feet, turned the Colt in his hand and swept the surrounding terrain with a long, probing glance. He saw nothing move, no other bronzed horsemen appear and he walked to the first lifeless form, retrieved his throwing knife and wiped it clean on the grass. He returned the knife to its calf holster and pulled himself onto the Ovaro and sent the horse northward. He'd just crested a low hill when he saw the cavalry platoon riding toward him at a fast canter and he saw the honey-wheat hair glistening in the sunlight alongside the officer at the head of the column.

He halted, waited and counted sixteen troopers as the platoon reached him. "First Lieutenant Baker," the young officer said as he waved the troop to a halt. Fargo took in a face that hadn't been shaving for too any years, an even-featured, serious face that tried to make earnestness hide its youth.

"Don't stop on my account," Fargo said blandly. "Go on and see to those wagons."

"Move out," The lieutenant called to his platoon and Fargo saw the girl stay in place as the troopers swept past, her gray-blue eyes searching his face.

"I was afraid we'd find you'd been killed," she said.

"I don't kill easily," Fargo remarked.

"Are you coming along?" she asked.

"Why not?" Fargo shrugged.

"But you don't think there's any point in hurrying," the girl said.

"Go to the head of the class," Fargo replied.

"Why bother coming along?" she frowned.

"Curiosity," he said and saw her lips tighten.

"We'll talk later," she said and sent the light-brown mare into a fast canter after the platoon.

Fargo followed at a leisurely trot. He was in no hurry to see what he was certain they'd find and what he had seen all too often. He slowed as he rode past the lifeless forms of the two Indians that had attacked the girl, paused to look at the beadwork on their mocassins and the design on the armband of one of them. He nodded to himself, his mouth a grim line as he went on.